Also by Bella Forrest:

A SHADE OF VAMPIRE SERIES:

A Shade of Vampire (Book 1)

A Shade of Blood (Book 2)

A Castle of Sand (Book 3)

A Shadow of Light (Book 4)

A Blaze of Sun (Book 5)

A Gate of Night (Book 6)

A Break of Day (Book 7)

A Shade of Novak (Book 8)

A SHADE OF KIEV SERIES:

A Shade of Kiev

A Shade of Kiev 2

BEAUTIFUL MONSTER SERIES:

Beautiful Monster

Beautiful Monster 2

For an updated list of Bella's books,
please visit www.bellaforrest.net

Contents

Prologue: Kiev 1

Chapter 1: Kiev 5

Chapter 2: Kiev 9

Chapter 3: Kiev 13

Chapter 4: Kiev 19

Chapter 5: Kiev 23

Chapter 6: Mona 31

Chapter 7: Kiev 37

Chapter 8: Mona 41

Chapter 9: Kiev 45

Chapter 10: Kiev 55

Chapter 11: Mona 63

Chapter 12: Kiev 69

Chapter 13: Mona 73

Chapter 14: Kiev 75

Chapter 15: Kiev 77

Chapter 16: Mona 79

Chapter 17: Kiev 83

Chapter 18: Kiev 89

Chapter 19: Mona 93

Chapter 20: Kiev 97

Chapter 21: Kiev 103

Chapter 22: Mona 111

Chapter 23: Kiev 115

Chapter 24: Mona 121

Chapter 25: Kiev 123

Chapter 26: Mona 131
Chapter 27: Kiev 137
Chapter 28: Mona 141
Chapter 29: Kiev 147
Chapter 30: Mona 155
Chapter 31: Mona 159
Chapter 32: Mona 163
Chapter 33: Kiev 167
Chapter 34: Mona 171
Chapter 35: Kiev 175
Chapter 36: Mona 179
Chapter 37: Kiev 191
Chapter 38: Kiev 201
Chapter 39: Mona 205
Chapter 40: Kiev 209
Chapter 41: Kiev 213
Chapter 42: Mona 217
Chapter 43: Kiev 225
Chapter 44: Mona 227
Chapter 45: Mona 231

Prologue: Kiev

The beautiful Italian vampire stood by the port, gazing out at the ocean. The sight of her took my breath away. Even after centuries, she still had the same effect on me.

I approached quietly and placed a hand on her shoulder. She jumped back, extending her claws and lashing out as soon as she recognized me. I retreated a few steps, stunned by the hatred burning in her eyes.

"Stay away from me, you monster," she snarled.

Gone was the fear I had grown accustomed to seeing in her whenever I was in her presence. In its place was sheer malice.

Her words stinging my ears, I stared at her lips. Those soft red lips… Those lips that had once kissed me with passion. That had so often woken me from sleep. That had uttered words of undying love.

Those lips that had never used to require force or threats to press against mine.

But now, those lips cut me deep.

It was hard for me to reconcile how such venom could have emerged from such softness. Even though I knew I deserved every word.

Her insult penetrated my skin, seeped into my very bones and set my mind on fire. As I stared down at her, I caught the reflection of my own red eyes in hers. And I knew then that those lips would never kiss me willingly again, for what I had become could not evoke affection from anyone.

So I forced a kiss on her, as had become a habit of mine whenever I wanted to remind myself of her taste.

When she fought me, I gripped her neck and kissed her harder. I sank my fangs into her lower lip, drawing blood. Then I bit into her neck. Her gasping and struggling only added fuel to my frenzy. Aware of the crowd now gathering around us, I lifted my mouth from her skin and slammed her back against a tree. As I withdrew a dagger from my belt, she screamed. I clasped a hand over her mouth. Tears streamed down her cheeks as I ran the cold blade against her collarbone.

"Natalie Borgia," I whispered into her ear. "The vampires' ultimate diplomat. How will we manage without you?"

Her eyes widened as I cut a gash in her skin, her hands clawing against my shirt.

"Please! No… Kiev!"

"I think somehow we'll survive." The words escaped my mouth in a hiss, revealing what I had become: a snake.

"T-try to remember! Please. You don't want to do this."

I brought the dagger down and pierced her kneecap. My hand wasn't enough to stifle her shriek. I withdrew my hand as she gasped for breath, her eyes drowning in agony.

"That hurts, doesn't it? Good."

I slid the dagger out of her knee and waited a few moments. Then I brought it slamming down again, relishing the sound of bone splintering. Her hands reached for my neck. Returning the dagger to my belt, I wrestled her to the ground and straddled her hips.

Her lips had ripped out my heart.

Now I'll rip out hers.

Extending my claws, I dug deep into her chest. As my hand closed around her heart, I watched as she released her last breath. Then I placed my arms beneath her and lifted her onto my lap. I sat cradling her limp body against mine, as one would a child.

And I fell apart.

My body shook violently as tears streamed down my cheeks, mixing with the blood on my hands.

Chapter 1: Kiev

A searing pain brought me to consciousness. I reached for my stomach. Warm blood soaked my fingers. I looked up through the darkness of my cell to see a tall figure looming over me.

"We've come to a decision." The coarse voice of my captor echoed off the walls. "The execution will take place in three days."

"What?" I choked.

"We can't afford to keep you alive longer than that."

I gazed up at his face. Cold grey eyes stared down at me.

"You're making a mistake," I said, clenching my jaw against the pain.

"Mistake?" He let out a mirthful shriek. "Our only mistake has been not killing all of you vampires sooner."

He backed out of the cell and slammed the iron gate shut.

"Wait." I crawled to the bars before he disappeared. "Listen to me, Arron."

Large black wings rooted behind his shoulders shuddered as I uttered his name.

"You lost the right to address me as anything other than Master the day you betrayed me," he hissed. "Just be prepared. And don't fight when we come for you. It will only make things worse."

Before I could say another word, he left. His footsteps disappeared down the hallway. Retreating to the back of my cell, I leaned against the wall, gripping my abdomen. Blood still leaked from my wound. It was deep; the hawk had sliced me with his talons. Normally such a gash would have closed within seconds. But my body's natural healing capabilities weren't working as usual. The serum he had injected into me during my last lashing still flowed through my veins.

Seeking distraction, I cast my eyes around the prison. The cells closest to me were filled with vampires. Each of their pale faces shared the same terrified expression. Dark circles showed beneath their eyes: a sign that, like me, they had also been starved of blood. I knew that some of them were also traitors. But most were not. Clearly, our loyalty didn't matter to Arron any more. Being vampires was enough to qualify us for death.

I shouldn't have been surprised by Arron and his council's decision. It should have been obvious that our days were numbered as soon as my father declared war on their territory. But I had expected them to turn me into one of their kind. I would have been a useful addition to their army.

For months I had fantasized about the day when one of their witches would perform the ancient ritual that would forever rid me of the disease that was vampirism. Barely a day had passed since I had escaped from my father when I hadn't imagined myself as a hawk.

Sharp talons, heavy wings, a shining black beak… Unrecognizable.

The witch might even be able to change the color of my cursed red eyes.

So desperate was I to make this transformation a reality, I had traded myself in as an ally to the hawks. I had even stolen a newborn whom I knew was of particular value to them and handed him over. In exchange, they were to allow me to become one of them, and offer me protection in their realm.

But then I'd helped a girl escape. And in that moment of weakness, I'd willingly given it all up. I'd lost Arron's trust by allowing the humanity I silently craved to show through me.

Now that the hawks saw no reason to keep their end of the deal, death was a welcome prospect—it was better than falling back into the clutches of my father. I drew comfort knowing that the hawks had as much to lose as I did and would do all within their power to keep him locked out. But even still, three days seemed like far too long to wait.

The sooner they kill me, the better.

More footsteps sounded in the corridor, breaking through my thoughts. I crawled back to the bars and craned my neck to catch a glimpse of who was approaching. It was a young woman, pushing a wooden cart filled with sacks of blood.

"A last meal for those of you who remained loyal to Aviary," the servant called.

Snake blood, I was sure of it. Human blood was never wasted on us. I raised my nose in the air as she drew closer, taking in the scent of her own blood. Its subtle aroma mixed with the stench of the reptile blood.

She moved from cell to cell, handing out sacks through the bars. After unloading the final one, she pushed the empty cart back toward the exit. I pulled myself into standing position against the bars of my cell, waiting for the moment she would pass by.

If this was to be my last chance of human blood—my last chance of pleasure before my time ended—I wasn't going to fight my darkness. All would be black soon anyway.

As soon as she was close enough, my arms shot out. Placing one hand around her throat and the other around her waist, I slammed her back against the gate. As I struggled to position myself to sink my teeth into her neck through the bars, pain stabbed me.

Swearing, I released her.

She staggered back, anger flickering in her deep blue eyes. She wiped my blood from a small dagger onto the hem of her short brown dress. Sliding it into a leather sheath, she tucked it into her bosom. She flicked a strand of long dark-blonde hair away from her face, and after glaring at me for several moments, she resumed her place behind the cart and continued toward the exit.

Feeling dizzy, I knelt on the ground. I wasn't sure which wound to apply pressure against now.

Blasted slave.

"You don't want to mess with that one," a voice whispered. I raised my eyes to a female vampire in one of the cells opposite mine. "She belongs to Arron. You're not going to make things any easier for yourself when the time comes."

The vampire paused for a moment, eyeing me and wiping blood away from her mouth. Despite having shared the same prison as me for several days, this was the first time she had spoken to me.

"What's your story?" she asked.

I shook my head and remained silent. I had no desire to dwell on the horrors of my past at this late hour of my life.

Chapter 2: Kiev

I tried to fall asleep again, but failed. My body ached too much. I couldn't lie on my back due to the lashings I'd received at the hands of Arron, and now I couldn't rest on my stomach either. There was barely a patch on the floor that wasn't moist with my blood. The stifling humidity and smell of rotting wood that engulfed the whole prison didn't help to ease my discomfort.

Instead, I found myself listening to a conversation that had broken out between some of the prisoners in the nearby cells.

"What do you think they'll do to the humans?"

"Once the Elders arrive, having humans around will be too much of a risk."

"Yes. It won't take much for the Elders to procreate... turn the humans into vampires."

"Maybe Arron will want some of the humans turned into hawks. As for the rest, it will probably just be easier to kill them off."

"Damn, I wish they'd give that job to us. I'd murder a baby for some human blood right now."

I tuned in and out of the conversation, attempting to discover that peaceful place between sleep and consciousness. I was disturbed by a loud crash coming from the direction of the prison entrance.

"He warned you!"

I opened my eyes to see another hawk standing in the hallway. Armor covered his chest. A guard. He was gripping Arron's servant girl by the neck.

"Spend a night or two rotting down here and then see if you prefer it in his chambers."

He grimaced as he swung open the door of an empty cell in the row opposite mine and shoved her inside. I noticed a thin cut beneath his left eye. He stormed away, allowing me a full view of the girl. Her right cheek was swollen and she had a bloody gash near her collarbone. The smell of her blood made my stomach groan. I cursed the hawk beneath my breath for placing her so close to me.

She had a stony expression on her tan heart-shaped face as she shuffled further into her cell until her back hit the wall. Perhaps sensing me watching her, she looked up and held my gaze for a few seconds before scowling and looking back down at her knees.

"Your little knife trick didn't work on him then?" I said, unable to contain my irritation first at the wound she had inflicted on me, and now her torturing me with her presence.

She kept her focus determinedly on her knees.

A speck of her blood on the floor caught my attention. It had fallen to the ground just outside my cell in her scuffle with the hawk. I extended a hand through the bars and scooped it up with my finger. Tasting it was probably the most foolish thing I could have done; it should only have made my cravings ten times worse. But strangely, this blood didn't have me craving more the way a human's normally would. It certainly tasted better than reptile blood, but it didn't have the same succulent quality that human blood had.

"What are you?" I peered at her.

She remained silent.

I thought back to what now seemed like a previous life and tried to recall the taste. I soon found the memory I was seeking. On my father's bidding, I had once tortured one of her kind.

"You're not human, are you?"

"No," she snapped.

"You're a witch."

She didn't answer, but I knew I was right.

I didn't speak again for several hours. But when I looked up to see that she was still awake, afraid that I was losing my mind to the pain, I distracted myself with her again.

"So, if you're a witch, why do you let him treat you this way? Why don't you fight back?"

"What's it to you?" she muttered.

"Oh, I have no interest in you. I'm just trying to take my mind off of my impending death."

At that, she fell silent. But after several minutes she said quietly, "I can't wield magic."

"You're not a witch then?"

"I *am* a witch," she sighed, as though this was an explanation she had repeated to many people before. "But I was born without powers."

"Why?"

"Why were you born with horrible red eyes? These things just happen."

I averted my eyes to the ground, wincing at her words.

"I don't belong here," she whispered. The tone of her voice was urgent, causing me to look at her again. She crawled closer to the bars. It dawned on me then that she was quite attractive without furrowed brows and a scowl.

"That makes two of us." I grimaced.

"I've only been in this hell-hole a few weeks. I… I'm a wanderer. A pirate. I left my crew to come to these shores to collect fruits."

"That was foolish of you."

"I've made the trip dozens of times before without getting caught. It's just this time…" Her voice trailed off for a few minutes before she found it again. "I've been holed up with these monsters ever since."

"Why are you telling me all this? If I knew a way out, I wouldn't be sitting here in a pool of my own blood—"

I stopped mid-sentence.

My stomach twisted into knots. My heart skipped a beat. A paralyzing feeling of dread swept over me. I gazed around the room, trying to make eye contact with any vampire looking my way. From their panicked expressions, they had sensed it too.

A dark presence that was felt but never seen. A presence that we all knew too well.

An unbearable cold seeped into the core of my bones—a sensation that never failed to make me pray for death.

It was too late.

My father had returned for me.

Chapter 3: Kiev

A haze descended over my eyes, making my vision slightly unfocussed.

"I've missed you, son." A hiss echoed in my head. "But you have disappointed me. Have you forgotten all I've done for you?"

No, I thought.

"You were one of the first humans I ever infected with our nature. One of my first mutations. With that comes responsibility. I gave you power when you had none. I made you immortal. I gave you these red eyes. Don't ever forget that."

I can't.

"I trusted you. And you betrayed me in the worst way imaginable. You sacrificed my trust to join our sworn enemies. You understand that such behavior cannot go unpunished."

I understand.

Though his words caused my mind to erupt in panic, I couldn't help but wonder how in hell they'd managed to penetrate Aviary so quickly.

"Oh, Kiev," his voice replied in my head, having read my mind. "You should know better than to underestimate the cunning of the Elders after so many years under my wing. We have our ways… but I have more important matters to set your mind on now."

My body moved toward the bars and my head turned from side to side, surveying the prison. The witch recoiled, her eyes wide with shock.

"You want to escape this place, don't you? Well, I've come to rescue you, my son. Fear not. We'll find a way out of here…"

My father moved my body to the darkest corner of the cell. I sat rigidly upright for what felt like hours. From the translucent appearance of their eyes, the other vampires had also been inhabited by the evil spirits that called themselves Elders. The original vampires. Except for the female vampire opposite me. Like the witch, she cowered in a corner of her cell.

Silence engulfed the prison. The only sounds that could be heard were the wind against the trees outside and the intermittent dripping of water on wood.

Since escaping my father, I'd tried to lock away the nightmares of all the years I'd spent under his influence. Now that he had reclaimed my body, memories flooded back. An entire village slaughtered. The blood of a child soaking my hands. My love, Natalie, screaming her bruised lungs out as I tortured her to death.

It felt as if the Elder was swallowing up any glimmer of hope for redemption I had been trying to kindle in a small corner of my soul. He was pulling me down into the pit of night I was trying to clamber out of.

My ears picked up a clinking of keys in the distance, then the thudding of dozens of footsteps. I had lost all track of time, but our three days must have been up. Either that, or the hawks had decided to come for us earlier.

"Keep a close eye on them." Arron's voice sounded out. "Most of them are weak by now, but desperation has a way of giving strength. I'm going to see to my slave first."

Arron unlocked the witch's cell and pulled her out. A dozen other hawks entered my line of vision and began unlocking gates. With us in the shadows, they didn't even notice our faces until it was too late.

I lunged forward with strength I didn't know my body still possessed. All vampires struck at once, taking the hawks by surprise. Before he had a chance to fight back, I bit into a guard's neck, tearing out his throat with my fangs and finishing the job with my claws.

I whirled around to see the prison in instant chaos: vampires and hawks flailing as they battled against each other, screams and shrieks piercing the atmosphere.

Arron screeched. He let go of the witch and flew toward me. I rushed forward and when we clashed, I was surprised that my already broken body didn't shatter to pieces. My claws lashed out, aiming for his eyes. He beat his wings and, gripping both of my hands in his talons, raised me into the air. Just as Arron poised himself to strike me with his sharp beak, the haze cleared from my eyes and the chill within my bones seeped out of me.

Arron looked at me with alarm. Without warning, he let go of me. I fell ten feet to the ground.

Across the prison, the female vampire who had not yet been inhabited now stood rigidly with her eyes rolling in their sockets. My father must have seen her in a more advantageous position.

As I lay aching on the floor, Arron's servant took advantage of the pandemonium and darted toward the exit of the prison. I forced my wrecked body to stand up. Keeping close to the wall and moving as fast as I could, I stayed within the shadows and exited the prison after her. Once out in the fresh air, I turned back to check the entrance of the prison—a square windowless building made of wood. Like all the constructions in Aviary, it had been built in the treetops, hundreds of feet above the jungle undergrowth. I heaved a sigh of relief to see that nobody had followed me yet.

My ears picked up the crack of a branch. I ran to the edge of the platform as a dark blonde head disappeared beneath the thick canopy of leaves about ten meters below. I hurled myself over the railing, hoping I wouldn't impale myself on a sharp branch.

On falling through the upper layer of leaves, my body made contact with a thick branch that I scrambled up on before tumbling down toward the jungle's undergrowth. The witch was still scurrying down the tree as if she hadn't noticed me. But she was slow, and limping.

"Wait!" I hissed.

I caught up with her and she let out a small scream. I placed a hand over her mouth to stifle it.

"I am not going to hurt you."

"Stay away from me!"

She pulled my hand away from her face and continued climbing down the branches, wincing with every movement she made.

I dropped myself down directly beneath her, blocking her next step.

"Where are you going?" I asked. She attempted to push me out of the way, but I gripped her arms and held her in place. "Do you know a way out of here?"

She let out a dry laugh. "As if I would tell you!"

A shrill scream sounded overhead, and then a rustling of leaves, close to us. She looked at me, desperation clouding her better judgment.

"I need to get to my boat. I'm sure it's still moored on the beach about a mile away from where I was caught."

"Climb onto my back," I ordered.

She narrowed her eyes on me. "Why would I do that?"

I considered just taking her by force rather than wasting time arguing, but I had a better chance of escaping with her cooperation.

"Listen, witch. You said you have a boat. If I don't escape this place, I face death or worse. I'm not going to hurt you because I *need* you."

I held out my hand, my eyes drilling into hers, urging her to take it. She hesitated, her dark blue irises filled with fear and uncertainty. But then her warm hand clasped mine. I turned around so that my back faced her. Her weight slid onto me and she wrapped her legs around my waist. I clenched my jaw against the pain of her body brushing against the open wounds Arron had slashed into my back, and hurried downward.

"Faster!" Her breath was hot against my ear.

When my feet hit the ground, she pointed to my right. "That way!"

I lurched forward and continued to follow her directions, dodging the giant snakes that writhed in the undergrowth. More screeches echoed down from above. We both looked around, but nobody appeared to be following us. *The hawks and Elders must still be keeping each other busy.*

Soon enough, the salty breeze blowing through the trees was unmistakable. When we emerged on a rocky shore, the sun hit me and my skin erupted in pain. But I had no choice but to keep moving forward. I ran for about half a mile before we found what she was looking for.

"Down there." She pointed to an area enclosed by rocks where a small boat was moored. I was relieved to see that it had a roof over it. I jumped down the rocks and leapt into the boat. As soon as the witch slid off my back, I retreated to the shadiest spot I could find.

"Oh, no. My engine!" The witch walked to the edge of the boat and cast her eyes around the empty waters. Fully clothed, she dove into the sea.

She swam around, ducking her head beneath the water and making strange moaning sounds. Then she disappeared completely. When she showed no signs of emerging after two minutes, I began to consider diving in after her. But then her head bobbed up above the water, followed by two sea creatures. I blinked several times. They were two large blue dolphins.

She guided both of them to the front of the boat and strapped them into thick leather harnesses. Catching hold of the reins, she hauled herself back onto the boat, joining me beneath the roof.

"I knew they wouldn't abandon me," she muttered to herself.

She tugged on the reins and we lurched forward at such a speed that it was hard to breathe for a few moments. I turned to face her. Her eyes were forward, concentrating on the open sea ahead, as though strapping reins on dolphins was the most normal thing in the world.

"What's your name, vampire?" she asked.

"Uh, Kiev Novalic. Yours?"

She kept her gaze ahead.

"Mona. Just Mona."

Chapter 4: Kiev

The fabric of my torn shirt irritated my singed skin. I removed it and threw it overboard. I found a bucket in a corner of the boat and, dipping it into the ocean, emptied it over my head. The salt stung, but at least the water was cool.

"Where are we going?" I asked.

"The nearest place I can get rid of you."

Her tone grated on my nerves. I was still keenly aware of the throbbing in my arm and my throat was parched for blood. At that moment, it took all the willpower I had to not sink my fangs into her neck. My survival was still dependent on her cooperation, so I had no choice but to rein in my annoyance and maintain a civil tone.

Dripping wet, I sat down next to her on the small bench in the center of the boat and turned to face her. She kept her eyes on the ocean.

"And where might that be?" I asked.

"The Cove. It's also where I left my ship and crew. About a day away, providing Kai and Evie keep up their current speed."

We had just entered a particularly rough set of waves and sitting on the bench became uncomfortable. I moved to the floor and looked up at her, now closer to her line of vision.

"What's The Cove?"

"Home of the merfolk."

Her answer was interesting to me on many levels. I was curious about the world outside of Aviary. I had lived on Earth for the majority of my life, at The Blood Keep—the Elder's castle. Only recently had I travelled through the portal into this strange parallel realm of supernaturals. Even my experience of Aviary, the country of hawks, was limited—not to speak of all the other hundreds of territories ruled by different supernatural races.

"I wouldn't expect a hearty welcome from them," the witch continued. "In fact, you'd be hard pressed to find a single race that embraces the spawn of the Elders with open arms."

"Will I be any better off there than in Aviary?"

"Maybe. Maybe not. Whatever the case, it's your problem."

I breathed deeply.

"But is there shade there? You need to at least leave me somewhere I can find shelter from the sun."

"I'll drop you near a cave," was all the assurance she gave me.

A particularly violent wave slammed my back against the side of the boat. I groaned, cursing the witch in my head for being unable to heal me with magic.

"That serum won't be in your blood forever. I suspect it'll be gone within a day. Just get some sleep. You're going to need it." She gave me a sour smile. "And I could do without your voice in my ears for a few hours."

I didn't know how I managed to fall asleep in that cramped corner of the boat, with the ocean knocking me about. But eventually, my body gave in to slumber.

Chapter 5: Kiev

My stunning human captive stood in my bathroom, undressed from the waist up. On seeing me enter, she reached for a towel and clutched it against her chest. I walked over and stood behind her, slipping my hands beneath her towel and running them along her skin. I shivered as I drew warmth from her pregnant body.

"Please, Kiev," she choked, flinching at my touch. "Let me go. I can't survive this without my husband."

On mention of Derek Novak, I stopped caressing her and settled my hands over her protruding stomach.

"I told you to forget that man."

"I can't. I won't."

I gripped her abdomen tighter, applying pressure with my fingers.

"If you want your twins to be born alive," I whispered into her ear. "I suggest you heed my warnings."

"Please. If you let me escape this place, I'll do anything…willingly."

The anguish in her voice made me take a step back. My gaze roamed the length of her body before meeting her glistening green eyes. Her beauty made me ache inside.

Anything? I began to mull over all the things I wanted to do with her at that moment. The possibilities were endless…

I was shocked when she took my hand and pulled me into the bedroom, toward the bed. She lay between the sheets and looked up at me with a determined expression on her face even while tears brimmed in her eyes.

"If this is what you want from me," she whispered. "I'll give it to you."

If you don't take her now, *I thought to myself.* You're going to regret it forever.

Brushing aside her long auburn hair, I pulled myself over her and leaned toward her neck. I breathed in her intoxicating scent before running my tongue along her bite marks, licking away the dried blood. It felt like no matter how much of her blood I drank, I would never be satiated.

Standing up, I looked into her eyes again for a reaction. They looked docile. Jaded. For as long as I had known her, Sofia Claremont had never given into my demands without a fight. Now, her surrender to my darkness unnerved me.

"You don't want me," I muttered after several minutes. "You're just desperate."

She looked up at me, her eyes widening. Perhaps she believed it to be an act of mercy. If only she had known that what I had planned for her was the furthest thing from merciful.

I woke up in a sweat. Night had fallen and the boat had stopped moving. I sat up, noticing that the pain in my body had subsided. I ran my hands along my skin. It felt smooth. Mona had been right. The sleep had done my body good. How long I had been sleeping, I could only guess.

I stood up and looked around the empty deck.

"Witch?" I called.

Splashing came from the waters nearby. Over the edge of the boat, two shiny heads bobbed above the waves. And the witch. She sat with her legs on either side of one of the dolphins, her wet dress hiked up her toned thighs, blood around her lips, nimbly picking apart a fish with her bare hands.

"They needed to stop for dinner," she said.

I was ravenous. Even the sight of fish blood made my stomach grumble. I slid into the cool waters.

"How do you catch those things without a net?" I asked, swimming toward her.

"Kai might be able to spare you one, if you ask him nicely." She patted the dolphin on the head. It lifted its shiny face from the water, opening its mouth to reveal several squished fish.

The smell made me feel nauseous. Ignoring her insult, I turned away and ducked beneath the waves. I opened my eyes, and immediately felt like a fool. The salt stung my eyeballs. *Clearly it's been too long since I've swum in seawater.*

I had no choice but to rely on my sharp sense of hearing. I held my breath and ducked down again. A school of fish swam about ten feet away from me. I kicked hard and pushed myself downward, my claws outstretched.

I resurfaced with nothing.

Mona eyed me. Unwilling to let her watch me make a spectacle out of myself, I swam to the other side of the boat where I was out of her view. I took a deep breath and dove deep once again. I continued failing. After several more attempts, I gave up.

As I returned, Mona looked at me, a hint of amusement in the corners of her lips. She strapped what appeared to be a set of waterproof glasses over her eyes. I had no idea how she would have gotten hold of such an object. Withdrawing a thin dagger from her belt, she pressed her heels against the dolphin's body and they both disappeared beneath the waves. Several moments later, they resurfaced, three large fish pierced through with Mona's dagger. She handed the blade to me and I was too hungry to refuse out of pride. I dug my fangs into the fish.

"That's about as far as my hospitality goes," she muttered, watching me drink.

Once I'd finished, I dipped my head in the water to clean my mouth. Looking at her still eating, I was keenly aware of how much tastier a morsel she would have been. Thinking it wise to distance myself from the temptation, I swam back to the boat and lifted myself up onto its edge.

"Why do you live like this?" I asked, staring at her.

"Huh?"

"Why don't you live with your kind in The Sanctuary?"

She averted her eyes to the water. A few moments passed before she cleared her throat, wiping blood away from her mouth with the back of her hand.

"I prefer freedom over comfort," she said.

"Have you always lived this way?"

"For a long time."

Although she appeared to be in her early twenties, her eyes told a different story. Something about them told me that she had undergone more suffering than any twenty-year-old should have. They were jaded. Fearful. Untrusting.

She finished her fish, guided the dolphins back into their harnesses and pulled herself onto the boat. I joined her on the bench where she grabbed the reins and urged her pets forward. As the wind caught her long hair, it brushed against my face.

"You've asked me questions," she said. "And since we've still got some journey ahead of us, I suppose it's my turn. So tell me, who are you?"

Who am I?

I could think of many descriptions for myself, for my life that had thus far been defined by my father. *Murderer* was the first word that came to mind, but clearly not the wisest choice of answer given the circumstances.

"Just a man who had the misfortune of bumping into a hungry vampire," I found myself saying.

I was sure that Arron wouldn't have had any reason to discuss my history with a slave. There was no way she could have known that I was putting on an act.

There was no way she could have known that, in reality, I was an unpredictable monster who could have blackouts at any moment. Who could regress into uncontrollable states of violence that were still very much a part of my being, thanks to my father's long reign over me. I recalled my last night with Natalie. She had tried to make me remember what we used to have. And her attempts to appeal to my humanity had made me break down and lose myself completely.

I'd tortured her to death.

No, there was no way Mona could have known that I was a bomb with a faulty fuse.

Besides, I would be gone from her life soon, and she would never see me again.

"How come you ended up in Aviary?" Her eyes turned on me suspiciously.

"I'd been a prisoner at the hawks' headquarters in the human realm while Arron was visiting. He brought me back to Aviary along with a dozen other vampires," I said.

I felt confused as to why exactly, but I didn't want her to know that I was a coward. I wasn't proud of stealing a newborn from his helpless mother, knowing that he would be of value to Arron.

I had supposed that the only place I would be safe from my father was in the realm of his fiercest adversaries. So desperate was I to escape his clutches, I hadn't given any thought to the quality of life I might have there. Any place away from the Elder's reach would give my soul a gasp of air, no matter how toxic that air might be.

"So you've been a victim of Arron too, huh," she muttered darkly, gazing back out at the ocean.

I didn't need any imagination to guess the type of things he would have tried to get Mona to do. Because I wasn't any less wicked a man than Arron.

"Why did he list you as one of the vampires I shouldn't give a last meal of blood to? What did you do to betray him?"

"It was… over a human girl…" My voice trailed off. Pain settled in my chest just thinking of Sofia. "A human girl I cared for. Perhaps even loved. I let her escape back to the human realm before all the hawks' portals were finally sealed off."

Mona's deep blue eyes reflected the moonlight as she turned to face me, her eyebrows arched. "That was brave of you. Selfless even. I didn't get the impression that you were capable of such finer emotions after what you tried to do back in the prison."

"I was desperate. And starving. I barely knew what I was doing."

What the hell am I doing? Why am I trying to defend myself?

I felt shocked by my reaction. I didn't know why I was trying to paint a picture of myself as someone decent and virtuous. As someone capable of love.

Why do I care what she thinks of me?

Or perhaps I don't...

Maybe all this is my subconscious showing through. Maybe, now that I might have a chance to carve out a life of my own away from my father's shadow, it's portraying the person I want to be. The person I had hoped the human girl could have made me.

Perhaps I do prefer light over darkness.

I couldn't deny that my mood swings had reduced since I first escaped my father. Without his presence, I'd found more room for my own thoughts in my head. I'd had a chance to experiment controlling my own willpower.

I wondered then, if I practiced being someone else every day for long enough, whether that could eventually become reality. I might have failed at changing my appearance, but if nobody knew who I was at The Cove, maybe that didn't matter.

Can an actor ever truly become the part he plays?

Do I want it enough?

"Well," the witch sighed. "I'm not convinced you're not just saying all this to warm me up. I'm still dropping you off at The Cove."

Again, her words made me feel like punishing her for her audacity. I wanted to maim her. Instead I just nodded. I looked out at the endless expanse of water rushing past us, taking in deep breaths.

"How did you train those things?" I asked.

"Things? You mean my dolphins? I was taught by a mermaid."

"Are there many others like you?"

"A fair number. We tend to move around in groups. Our chances of survival are obviously better that way." She paused and ran her tongue over her lower lip. "But honestly, I keep to myself most of the time. My group is large enough to allow me to do that. I'm a wanderer in the true sense of the word. I don't like the commitments that form when you're around people for an extended period of time."

Asking her aimless questions was distracting my mind from her blood, so I continued.

"Do you have family?"

"Dead." She said the word without a hint of emotion. "Do you?"

My parents had died while I was still a human. I'd been a young boy when an epidemic had swept through our town centuries ago, taking them with it. As for my younger brother and sister, after my turning, I'd never seen them again.

"No," I said.

But the words felt strange as I said them. For so long my Elder had forced me to address him as my father, and his other children as my siblings, that it was ingrained in me that I should still be acknowledging them as family.

Pull yourself together, Kiev. You're away from him now.

You no longer have to live under his shadow. You have choice.

You can become whoever you want to be.

Chapter 6: Mona

I wondered why I had started talking so freely with this stranger. He didn't even seem interested.

Perhaps, despite all my attempts to convince myself otherwise, I was just desperate for someone to talk to. Perhaps I felt I could confide in this man, open up to him in ways I couldn't ever with anyone else, because I knew we would part ways in a few hours and I would never see him again.

Whatever the reason, I found myself answering questions about my life. Though I was always careful to skirt around the parts that were hidden too deep to reveal even to this complete stranger.

My hands became tired from holding the reins after a while. Normally I would stop Kai and Evie, but since Kiev agreed to hold them, we switched places. For a while, I placed my hands over his icy ones, guiding him on how to manage the dolphins. I tried to teach him to use the compass and explained when the dolphins were going too fast and what the optimal speed was. He was a fast learner and after half an hour, I was able to sit back and watch him take control.

Now that I wasn't navigating, I let my gaze fall on his face. I wasn't sure I would ever get used to his red eyes. They sent chills down my spine whenever he looked at me. They reminded me of the devil himself and made me hesitant to fall asleep. The moment I drifted off, those blood-red eyes would be watching me.

He had a strong jawline beneath his stubble, and his dark hair and eyebrows were at stark contrast with his pale skin. He was tall— almost a foot taller than me—and his body was strong and muscular, far too strong for comfort. He could easily overpower me should he decide to. My only assurance of safety was that he needed me to get to shore. If he killed me on board, he'd perish in the middle of the ocean. But that didn't stop him from eyeing me with hunger every now and then, sending shudders running through me.

I'd never been fond of vampires. I found it hard to trust creatures whose very existence depended on sucking the life out of others. And they were difficult to travel with. They were needy, craving human blood and complaining whenever they were given anything but. The only vampire I could stand was the captain of my ship, but perhaps that was just because I'd known him for so long.

"Tell me more about this group you're with," my passenger said, turning his bloody gaze on me.

"There are perhaps one hundred of us. Mostly vampires and werewolves."

He raised a brow at my statement.

"I didn't really end up with them by design." I sighed. "I've known the captain of our troop for years. I met him soon after leaving The Sanctuary. He and a werewolf saved me from a… difficult situation. Or you could say that we all helped each other. Anyway, since then we've stayed together. And gradually we picked up more people along the way, until the crew became what it is today."

"Vampires and werewolves," he muttered. "I never knew the two races could live in harmony."

I smirked at the notion. "Oh, they have their fair share of squabbles. But in general, vampires and werewolves can work well together … at least compared to other supernaturals. We've tried adding other races to our crew in the past—ogres, mermaids, ghouls—but it rarely worked out. While wolves and vamps certainly aren't the best of friends, if they have a shared goal, they are at least functional."

He leaned back in his seat and placed his feet up on top of an empty water barrel. There was an awkward silence as he continued to look me over. I wondered what he was thinking: whether he actually wanted to join our group, or if he was just asking questions because he was bored.

"Is it really so bad in The Sanctuary?" he asked abruptly. "From what I've heard, it's a place of freedom if you're a witch—"

I guessed that his question wasn't asked maliciously, but it hit a nerve so raw it sent tremors tearing through my entire body.

"I've had enough of your questions!" The words rolled out of my mouth before I could stop them.

He fell silent.

I immediately regretted losing my temper. I'd been secretly enjoying interacting with him. Now I felt guilty.

"I'm sorry… I actually don't mind you asking questions. It helps to pass the time. I-I'm just starting to feel tired."

"I'm not stopping you from sleeping," he snapped.

For some reason, I didn't want to risk upsetting him by saying that I didn't trust him enough to close my eyes. Perhaps I was worried it would deter him from speaking to me freely.

I questioned why I didn't want to fall asleep. I was certainly exhausted; I hadn't slept properly for days. Of course it was true that, although he could follow the basic direction of a compass, he didn't know where our ultimate destination was and he needed me to oversee his navigation.

But I felt within myself a resistance that was distinct from and deeper than this. I didn't want to waste the short period of time I had remaining with him on sleep. I doubted I'd ever meet another stranger in such short-lived circumstances again.

"No, I need to make sure you don't steer off course. I'll be okay." Eager to divert the topic away from the witches' realm, I blurted out the first thing that came to my head. "So why are your eyes red? I know I said you were born with them, but I'm guessing that's not true since you were born a human. I've never seen a vampire with red eyes."

He looked out at the ocean, almost as though ashamed of his appearance. He didn't answer my question.

I cast my eyes out of the boat too and scanned the waters. My breath hitched as I caught sight of a tiny island, the first landmark indicating the proximity of the mermaids' territory. We were perhaps an hour away now. A strange panic gripped me. I wasn't used to time passing so quickly, especially not on sea journeys.

Before I could stop myself, I found myself asking, "Tell me about the human girl you fell in love with. Was she your first love?"

A muscle in his jaw twitched.

"That's none of your business."

"Please," I urged, wincing at how desperate I sounded.

He frowned at me. "No, she wasn't," he said.

"What was her name?"

Again he scowled and kept his lips sealed.

"What's it like to fall in love?"

He shot me a look, perhaps wondering if this was supposed to be some kind of joke. "Are you always this aggravating?"

The truth was, I felt as confused by my behavior as he looked. This wasn't *me*.

But as I allowed myself to pause and search a little deeper into my soul, I realized. This was a question that I couldn't ever discuss with anyone else without risking becoming on closer terms with them. A question that had run deep within me ever since I could remember. A question that I had never gotten out of my system. A question that would likely go unanswered for the rest of my life if I didn't ask it of this stranger before he left my boat.

"Just answer my question… please."

I snatched the reins from him and slowed the dolphins.

"What the hell are you doing?" he asked, anger rising in his voice.

"Answer my question," I repeated, trying to keep the tremors of desperation out of my voice. Embarrassment rose in my cheeks.

Breathing deeply, he stood up and turned his back on me.

"It's not worth it."

"What do you mean?" His answer had thrown me off. "So you fear love?"

"Yes," he said, after a pause. I was surprised by his admission. "And no. Somehow, even with the pain, it reminds you that you're still living."

"And what do you fear?"

He crossed his arms over his chest and remained silent for several moments. I stared at him, barely blinking.

"Numbness," he said finally. "Now will you keep moving?"

Numbness.

Chapter 7: Kiev

I let out a sigh of relief as the shores of what appeared to be an island came into view. *The sooner I rid myself of this witch, the better. I don't know how much longer I can keep myself from clawing at her.* I stepped outside the cabin to get a better look. Although the darkness was still very much prevalent, the horizon displayed signs of the sun about to peek through. I gazed up at the clear sky.

My breath hitched.

A large bird-like figure circled in the far distance. Then my eyes fell on the beach. Hawks roamed there too.

I rushed back into the cabin.

"Stop! Turn around!"

"What?" Mona said.

"Hawks!"

Mona frowned. Then she let out a dry laugh. "Do you really think I'm that stupid?" The boat continued to speed forward at a terrifying pace.

I grabbed hold of the reins and yanked them out of her hands, forcing the dolphins to a stop. She looked shocked and stood up, a new emotion traced in her night-blue eyes. Fear. I guessed what she was thinking; now I had caught sight of the shore, I no longer needed her.

"Fool!" I hissed. "Go see for yourself!"

She edged out of the cabin, her eyes not leaving me, as though I might pounce on her at any minute. I followed her outside and pointed toward the direction of the hawk in the sky, and also on the shore.

She rummaged around in a storage box and retrieved a large pair of rusty binoculars. On peering through them, she gasped. Dropping the binoculars, she rushed back into the cabin and grabbed the reins. She guided the dolphins into an about-turn and we sped off in the opposite direction.

"I hope they didn't notice us," she breathed.

The hawk was still circling in the same spot in the sky. He was showing no signs that he had spotted us.

"What now?"

She ignored me, a deep scowl settling in on her face.

"No. No. No," she muttered to herself beneath her breath. Her cheeks had turned red.

I was content with not having an answer immediately so long as we continued to speed away from The Cove. She closed her eyes and clenched her jaw, rubbing her forehead with her palm furiously.

"I just hope that my crew left in time," she croaked. "Before the hawks took control of the place."

"But why? What interest do they have in the merfolk?"

"Your guess is as good as mine," she said darkly. "Aviary is now a nation at war. The Cove is the nearest major realm to Aviary.

Perhaps they believe that securing that place will assist in some way in their battle with the Elders… though I doubt the merfolk allowed themselves to be held hostage. I'm sure the majority of them will have abandoned their homes and moved to deeper waters…"

She stopped, overcome by a deep yawn. I looked over and saw the look of sheer exhaustion in her face.

"You still haven't told me where we're headed now," I said. "But I don't trust you to navigate us anywhere in this state."

"No, no, I'm"—she tried to stifle another loud yawn with her hand—"fine."

"If it's me you're worried about, you're a fool," I said. "I still need you. I'd have no idea where to even start now."

She glanced up at me briefly and the hesitation in her eyes revealed that she was considering my words. I stood up and looked at the sky again. All signs of the hawk and the coast had vanished. Evie and Kai travelled with supernatural speed.

"All right. I suppose that we're a safe distance from The Cove," she said. "We can stop here for a few hours."

She still had a look of distrust in her eyes, but she seemed to understand her body would no longer allow her to deprive it of rest. She pulled the dolphins to a stop and tied the reins securely around a post. Rummaging around in a cupboard, she pulled out a small blanket and curled up on the bench, covering her face with the blanket.

I walked to a corner of the boat and sat down on the floor, leaning my back against the wall. Having nothing else to occupy my mind with, I watched her settle into slumber. She twitched now and then, until finally I could hear her soft even breathing.

As I sat there looking at her, I was surprised to find myself wishing that she hadn't tucked her face beneath the blanket.

Chapter 8: Mona

I didn't know how I managed to fall asleep with that monster sitting just a few meters away. I supposed my body simply gave me no choice.

When I woke up, I was shocked to see that it was dark again. I'd slept through the whole morning and the entire day. At least I felt refreshed. But the thought of being so vulnerable to the vampire for so long terrified me.

I slowly moved the blanket away from my face, afraid to look up and be met with blood-red eyes glinting at me through the darkness. But the vampire had vanished from the cabin.

My throat felt painfully dry. I stepped out onto the deck and headed over to the barrel of drinking water. It was stale now, having been on the boat for so many weeks, and there were barely a few cups left. I could have drunk the whole lot in one go, but I had to pace myself. We were only a few hours away from our next destination, but I couldn't run out of drinking water in case something else threw us off course. Drinking seawater wouldn't make me ill like it would a human, but I hated the taste. Fortunately, my vampire companion didn't seem to drink water at all.

"Hello?" I called.

I walked over to the edge of the boat and peered into the water. To my horror, both dolphins were out of their harnesses. Kiev was floating nearby.

"What are you doing?"

I dove into the water and rushed toward them.

"They were hungry," he said coolly. "And since you decided to sleep for so long, I didn't want this journey to be further delayed by their meal."

"But you don't know how to manage them," I panted. "They don't answer to you like they do to me! You do realize that if we lost them, we'd be—"

"They seem to be answering to me quite well, don't they?" He gestured to both of the dolphins, who were happily chewing away on mouthfuls of fish. "You underestimate me, witch. I'm a fast learner."

I reached Evie and pulled myself onto her back, glaring at Kiev.

"I don't care what you are. Just... don't touch them again without my permission."

I realized that I was also craving food. I withdrew my dagger and eye protection from my belt, and ducked down beneath the waves. I surfaced with two large fish. I glanced over at Kiev who was still eyeing me.

"Want one or not?" I asked.

He shook his head.

I split open a fish and started eating, tossing the other one over to Kai. He grabbed it in his jaws as soon as it hit the water.

"So, answer my question. What are we going to do now?" Kiev

said.

I fixed my eyes determinedly on my fish. I knew I couldn't delay answering him for much longer. Of course, I'd known exactly where we'd have to head the moment I'd realized Kiev had been telling the truth about the hawks at The Cove. The safest and nearest place was The Tavern. It was also the most likely place that my crew would have headed to, assuming they had managed to escape from The Cove before the hawks took over.

I finished chewing before answering. "A small island a few hours away. The Tavern."

"The Tavern," he muttered. "And whose territory is that?"

"Nobody's in particular."

"What do you mean?"

"It was founded by a group of pirates," I said. "They claimed the island as their own and built a wall around it. But over the years, it's become a place of respite for all wanderers and pirates."

"Will I be able to stay there permanently?"

"You'll be better off there than The Cove."

I'd already decided that I'd show him who to talk to once we arrived there in order for him to obtain permanent residency. And after that, he'd be their problem.

Just a few more hours to go.

I washed my face and led the dolphins back to their harnesses. Kiev and I resumed our seats on the boat. As we moved forward, I couldn't deny that part of me felt guilty that I hadn't offered to drop him at The Tavern to start with. It hadn't been that far out of my way. And it was without question safer for him than The Cove.

Of course I knew why I hadn't done it; I'd just wanted him out of my sight as soon as possible. I hadn't even given myself a chance to think of any alternatives to the merfolk's realm.

Now that the silence between us had returned, so did my embarrassment. Sitting so close to him didn't help. I doubted that I would have asked those personal questions of him had I known our journey would be delayed like this.

I felt thankful for the cool breeze wafting through the cabin, calming my blazing cheeks.

Chapter 9: Kiev

As soon as the silhouette of The Tavern came into view, Mona slowed the boat. I got up and stepped out on deck. I scanned the area for any sign of hawks. Nothing stuck out as suspicious to me.

A high black wall surrounded the island. Lanterns were scattered at intervals around it and an orange glow emanated up into the sky from behind the walls. Faint chattering and music drifted toward us.

I walked back to the cabin and resumed my seat next to Mona.

"It's safe," I muttered.

She nodded and we continued ahead at full speed until the dolphins approached shallower water and slowed down. When the boat hit the sand, we both jumped out. Mona loosed the dolphins from their harnesses and, to my surprise, let them go swimming off.

"I've trained them well enough. They'll stay around the area and be here when I need them again."

I helped Mona push the boat onto the sand. Wordlessly, she started walking toward the wall. I followed her, scanning the length of the structure. We were headed toward a large oak door carved into it. On approaching it, Mona knocked three times.

"Who is it?" a gruff voice shouted out from behind the door.

"Mona," she replied.

The door swung open. Standing in front of us was possibly the most grotesque creature I'd ever laid eyes on. His body was tall and wide, and his skin coarse like leather. Two small tusks grew out of his bottom jaw. His nose was squashed and small like a button. And one of his eyes was missing; the eye that remained was a bright orange color and bulged in its socket.

"Who's that?" he said, peering down at me curiously.

"It's okay. He's with me."

His face split into a crooked smile. "So Mona the witch finally got herself a man. About time." He broke out into raucous laughter.

"Shut it, Ronan," Mona snapped. "I'm just dropping him off here."

She pushed past the creature to escape his jeers. I sped by to catch up with her.

"What is that thing?" I asked, once I was sure we were out of earshot.

"An ogre," she muttered. "And don't be surprised. You get all sorts here."

We walked through a dark tunnel and up a dozen stone steps. We emerged into the borders of a town. Shabby buildings made of logs and bricks lined a wide dirt street. The place was lit with lanterns hanging from trees that gave off a warm glow.

Mona was right; an array of various creatures milled about. Vampires, werewolves and ogres were the only creatures I recognized. I tried to satisfy my curiosity about the others, but she ignored my questions, her eyes set firmly ahead as she sped forward. I couldn't help but notice how many of them had some kind of physical impairment, be it a missing leg or arm, or some other kind of disability. I even caught sight of some in makeshift wheelchairs.

I had no idea where Mona was leading me. She moved fast and dodged through crowds as she hurried forward.

Eventually we stopped outside a large stone building. "The Blue Tavern" was inscribed on a creaking wooden sign that swung above an old oak door. When we entered, bitter smoke invaded my nostrils, enough to induce a coughing fit. The lively tune of an accordion filled my ears.

A stout female vampire stood behind the bar taking orders. Mona asked for some water. The vampire turned her round face toward me and raised her eyebrows.

"You want something?"

I looked up at the menu scrawled on some wooden boards in white chalk. The most appealing thing on there appeared to be fish blood, which said a lot about the menu.

"No."

"Michelle, will you ask Elizabeth to come down briefly?" Mona asked. "I need to talk to her urgently about something."

Michelle nodded and said, "I'll check if she hasn't gone to bed already."

Mona thanked her and scanned the room. She walked toward the far corner of the room. We sat down at opposite ends of a creaking wood table. She took a sip of the water, her eyes on the table.

"You don't have to pay for that?" I asked.

"Payment in these parts is different to anything you're used to. As you'll soon find out."

She chugged down the glass of water in a few more gulps and left for a refill. She was gone for more than fifteen minutes and when she returned, she was accompanied by a large brown werewolf. It being night time, the wolf was in full transformation.

"Oh, hello," the wolf said on noticing me at the table. "Who are you?" Although the wolf's voice was gruff, I could still tell that this was a female.

"His name is Kiev," Mona answered for me.

The wolf reached out a paw to shake mine, her beady grey eyes gazing at me. I obliged her.

"I'm Saira," she said. "I take it that you're Mona's friend. Will you be joining our crew?"

"He's not my friend," Mona said. "I barely even know him." She said the words without looking at me. "And no. He won't be joining us. It's a long story, but I just agreed to drop him off here." She tapped her fingers on the table and craned her neck toward the direction of the bar. "I'm just waiting for Elizabeth so I can go up to bed…"

Barely had she said the words when a tall vampire wearing a long dress and an apron snaked her way around the tables and stood in front of Mona. She smiled briefly at each of us.

"Nice to see you again, Mona. How are you?"

"Fine, thanks. I'm actually planning to stay the night. Do you have an extra guest room available?"

"I'm sure we can arrange for that." Elizabeth pulled out a small ledger from her apron pocket and flipped through it. "Room forty is available. You can get the keys from Michelle behind the bar. Anything else you wanted?"

"Yes." Mona gestured toward my direction. "This vampire here… his name is Kiev Novalic. He wants to become a resident. I think you're the best person for him to speak to?"

Elizabeth looked me over before nodding her head. "Yes," she said. "I can assist with that."

"Good!" Mona sighed. She finished the rest of her second glass of water and stood up. "I'm going up to my room now."

"My room isn't far from yours," Saira said.

Mona didn't so much as glance at me as she nodded and left with the wolf. Elizabeth took a seat next to me and eyed me cautiously once again.

"Well," she said. "First of all I suppose I should welcome you to The Tavern, Kiev. Did Mona brief you at all on how things work here? Or should I start at the beginning?"

"You'd better start at the beginning."

"Very well." She cleared her throat and settled down into a more comfortable position in her chair. "I first need you to answer some questions about yourself. Who are you, where have you come from, and why do you want to stay here?"

Who am I?

That question again.

Who am I... or who do I want to be?

I settled for the same answer I'd given Mona. "I escaped from Aviary where I was being held hostage. I simply seek shelter, a place I can live without my life being at risk."

"Very well," Elizabeth said, peering at me from across the table. "Sounds simple enough. If you want to live here, you'll have to contribute. You'll have to take part in daily service, which can range from manning the gates, to fetching food, to helping with construction projects... Are you willing to be part of a community?"

"Yes," I said without thinking. "I'll do whatever it takes to be accepted here."

The truth was, absolutely anything sounded better than my previous existence. I really was willing to do whatever was required to give myself a chance to breathe and experience my own thoughts.

"That's what we like to hear." Elizabeth smiled. "Well, I suggest you get some rest now and I'll talk with you more about the details of your service tomorrow. I'll also go over the rules you must obey if you are to live here without getting into trouble. I'm too exhausted to go through all of that with you now. I've had a long day." She closed her ledger. "For tonight, we'll lodge you in one of the pub's guest rooms. But tomorrow, we'll move you to the vampires' quarters, which is much better suited to your needs."

She got up and led me over to the bar. "Hand me the key to room fifty-three please, Michelle. Oh, and is there a spare parasol somewhere behind the counter?"

Michelle handed her a key and a folded umbrella made of straw. We proceeded through a back door and up a winding staircase. We walked along several dim, carpeted corridors until we reached a small, tidy room that contained nothing but a single bed and a narrow window.

"Thank you," I said. "I think I'll take a walk before resting."

"As you wish." She handed me the umbrella. "Keep this for walking around in the daytime. It'll save you getting burned to a crisp."

With that, she left the room and shut the door behind her. I looked out of the window. The building wasn't high enough to allow a view of the sea. All I could see were large trees.

I left the room and headed downstairs. The pub was much emptier now, and as I stepped outside, so were the streets. I tried to remember where the door was that Ronan had let us through. I ended up asking a couple of vampires who were still out late. They soon pointed me in the right direction. When I reached the door, Ronan was slumped down in a chair sleeping, an empty bottle of rum on his lap.

Unwilling to wake him, I unlatched the door myself and stepped out, closing it behind me as silently as possible.

The fresh sea air blew against my face and I breathed in deeply. I could get used to living in a place like this. There were many people, but I had gotten the impression from Mona that not many were full-time residents. That would make it easier to blend in with the crowds. Notorious as I was back in the human realm, most vampires here wouldn't know me. *Hopefully this isn't just my wishful thinking.*

As I walked further along the beach, a bonfire blazed in the distance. A group of vampires sat around it, chatting and drinking. As I drew nearer, one of them shouted out.

"Who goes there?"

"Uh… a vampire," I called back.

"Yes, I can see that! What's your name?"

I paused for a moment before responding.

"Kiev."

A blond vampire with grey eyes got up and staggered toward me, a half-finished bottle of rum in one hand. He grabbed me by the shoulder and pulled me toward the group.

"Come join us!" he said with a grin.

Pulling away from him would have looked awkward, so I acquiesced. I sat down on the sand near the edge of the circle.

"Do you want some, Kiev?" the vampire nearest to me asked. He had a slight European accent. I looked up to see a dark-haired man— probably not much older than me—with warm brown eyes holding up a jug of rum.

I didn't trust myself in a sober state, let alone a state of intoxication.

"I don't drink," I said.

"Suit yourself." He smiled at me, topping up his own cup.

When I looked at him more closely, something about his appearance made my breath hitch. His dark features and warm brown eyes were eerily familiar.

"You're new here, aren't you?" His expression was that of mild curiosity.

"Yes."

"How are you liking it?"

"So far, it seems to be a welcoming place."

"That it is," he said. "Providing you follow the rules and don't push any boundaries, The Tavern is a safe place. One of the safest you'll find in these parts." He paused to take another sip from his cup. "What brings you here anyway?"

I repeated the same lie I'd told Mona and Elizabeth. I kept my explanation as brief as possible without sounding rude.

"Makes sense why you'd want to come here after that. Makes sense…" He nodded his head, his eyes glazing over a little. "I left the human realm a few centuries ago. I was taken to Cruor, the Elders' realm. Managed to escape during a raid by the hawks. Then Aviary eventually decided I wasn't useful to them. They let me go, and I've been a pirate ever since… I'm Matteo, by the way. Matteo Borgia. Pleased to meet you."

Borgia.

No.

It can't be.

He held out his hand. I shook it, fighting to conceal the shock that was now coursing through my body.

"Are you alone here, or with company?" he asked.

"Alone." My stomach writhed as I spoke. "Actually, I'm feeling exhausted from my journey. I'm going to head off."

"Of course." He patted me on the shoulder. "I'll be leaving the island soon, but I wish you the best of luck with everything."

I stood up and walked back toward the gate. As the group's chattering and laughter faded away in the distance, my mind still felt frozen with shock. I racked my brain for any indication of a relative named Matteo throughout the time I had known Natalie. She had once mentioned an older brother, but I didn't recall her ever telling me his name. If his surname and appearance were not some wild coincidence, and Matteo was indeed Natalie's brother, at least I could take comfort in one thing: he didn't know who I was. Which meant that there was a possibility he didn't even know that Natalie was dead.

I smiled bitterly. I had been hoping that this place would provide a fresh start. Seeing Matteo was like a splash of cold water. It instilled a chilling doubt in me that perhaps I never would escape the shadows of my past.

Still, as I reached my room and settled on the bed, I tried to convince myself that this was just a fluke. Matteo would be gone soon, and with him, the last painful reminder of the man I no longer wanted to be. I'd meet Elizabeth early the next morning and she'd assign me work.

Despite the shock of seeing Matteo, all in all, The Tavern still felt like the best option I had for recovery: a place where nobody knew who I was beneath the façade.

Chapter 10: Kiev

I woke to my skin stinging. I'd forgotten to shut the curtains the night before. The early morning sun's rays had just begun to stream into my room. I stood up and closed the curtains.

I was hungry again. I decided to go down to the bar to see if anyone could serve me breakfast. Even fish blood seemed tempting at that moment. I exited my room and locked the door behind me. I walked along the corridor and down the winding steps, but instead of proceeding directly to the ground floor, I stopped when I saw the sign for the fourth floor.

Room forty.

I could see it from where I was standing. I left the staircase and walked toward the room. The door was ajar. I knocked twice.

"Witch?"

No reply.

I pushed the door open. The room was empty, the bed sheets folded. There was no sign of any of her belongings. I wondered where she might have gone. But it was just as well. I doubted that I would have left the room without claiming at least a few gulps of her blood had she been there. And I didn't know how Elizabeth would have felt about that.

I pulled the door closed and continued down the staircase. Michelle was already behind the bar and looked up to greet me when I entered.

"Some eel blood," I said, even as I grimaced. "And do you know if Elizabeth is awake yet? I'm supposed to be meeting with her this morning."

"She should be down in less than an hour."

Michelle handed me a glass of blood and I made my way over to a table in the far corner of the room. I gingerly drank the blood and gazed around the empty pub. It appeared quite different now without the smoke and flickering lanterns. Tapestries made of snakeskin adorned the dark stone walls and skeletons of predatory fish hung from the low ceiling.

I looked back toward Michelle, sweeping the floors behind the counter.

"How did this place come to be?" I asked. Mona had never given me a satisfying explanation.

Michelle stopped sweeping and leant her large elbows on the counter.

"Well, that's rather a long story. But seeing as I'm down here early, I guess I can spare a few minutes to fill you in on some history."

Her smile was broad as she took a seat at my table. It paled slightly when I didn't return it.

"Long ago, this island was founded by a group of outcasts," she said, "or pirates as many call themselves. The group consisted of seven werewolves, ten vampires and two ogres, if memory serves me correctly. They'd finally grown tired of roaming the seas and wanted a base. They invited others to join them, and over the years, The Tavern has evolved to be a place of shelter for all kinds."

"Yet many don't live here full time?"

She nodded. "That's correct. Many enjoy the sea life. As for myself, I wouldn't be able to stand living on a boat and having nowhere to call my own."

"And who is Elizabeth exactly?" I asked.

"She's a relative of one of the original founders. As am I. Elizabeth and I are sisters, you see. We've helped run this place for years—"

"And why do people say it's so safe here?" I interrupted. "The wall is impressive, but I doubt it'd last five minutes if subjected to any real attack. What makes you think you're safe?"

"Well, because most of us are outcasts. We've already been rejected by other realms. We're not wanted. Of course, there are some who truly are rebels or escapees and left voluntarily, but for the most part, we've all been rejected for one reason or another. The other realms have little interest in what happens to us or what we get up to."

This was interesting to me. Mona had never described the situation like this; she had always spoken of herself as a rebel, a wanderer by choice. But now that I knew this, her having no magic and being a wanderer made perfect sense. Perhaps that was why she had been so upset with me when I'd questioned about why she wasn't better off living in The Sanctuary.

"But humans... surely they're of interest to the Elders?"

Michelle shook her head. "There aren't many humans here. And even those few who are here aren't of interest to any realm. They're contaminated."

"What do you mean, contamina—"

"They're either sick or there's something physically wrong with them that renders them useless."

I stared at Michelle. "And what about someone like me? Or Mona? Escapees."

"If the hawks wanted you, there's no reason they wouldn't come looking for you. It does happen. But Aviary is so wrapped up with Cruor, I honestly doubt they'd waste time looking for you." She paused and raised a brow at me. "Unless you really are that valuable to them."

Before I could say anything more, the front door swung open. Elizabeth walked toward us. She wore the same long dress with a white apron wrapped around her waist. Her grey-streaked hair was pulled tightly back in a bun. She nodded in my direction. Michelle left the table, and Elizabeth sat in her place.

"Good to see you up early, Kiev." She opened her book and ran a finger down one of the pages, mumbling to herself. "Aha, we do have a space there today. Good."

She shut the book and looked up at me.

"So, anyone wishing to stay at The Tavern for more than one week must contribute a minimum of five hours of work per day. Which isn't much when you think of what you get in return: protection that the Tavern offers, free board and lodging…"

I nodded.

"Given that you're a vampire," she continued, "you're obviously limited in the hours of day that you can work outside. So we'll allot you work accordingly. For example, this evening, I'm planning to send you for work on a new construction at the far end of the island. We're building some new housing to accommodate the influx of new vampires who've arrived here recently. I'll have someone come for you after sunset, so make sure you're around. They'll bring you to the building site and give you instructions as to your task."

I nodded again.

"After work, I'll have someone take you to your new accommodation in the vampires' quarter." She jotted something down in her book and then continued, "Next, as for important rules you must abide by if you are to avoid trouble—"

She was interrupted by a loud knock on the tavern front door. Elizabeth twisted in her chair to face the bar.

"Michelle!" she called.

Michelle had disappeared. Elizabeth sighed and walked toward the direction of the front door.

"We don't open until just before lunch! You know that," she called through the glass to whoever was knocking.

The knocking turned into banging. The door swung open and Elizabeth protested, "What are you doing, Jack? I told you, we're closed!" I strained my neck to see who it was but a pillar was obstructing my view.

"Which room is Kiev Novalic staying in?" a deep male voice asked.

I nearly choked on my drink.

"A tall vampire. Red eyes," he continued. "I know he arrived last night. Michelle said—"

"Yes, why do you want him? He's sitting over there."

I stood up. A man wearing a long dark cloak ran toward me. A human. I stood frozen to the spot, trying to place his face. But I couldn't; I had no idea who this man was or how he knew me. I extended my claws in anticipation. Arriving at the table, he slammed his fist down, leaving behind a rusting metal pendant.

"Do you recognize this, vampire?" His light blue eyes blazed into mine.

I recognized it immediately.

"I won't blame you if you don't," he scoffed. "You've likely murdered hundreds of innocents in the past few years."

He withdrew a sharp wooden stake from his cloak. Elizabeth gasped behind me.

"This pendant was my mother's," he shouted. "You murdered her five years ago."

It wouldn't have been difficult to overpower him, to knock the stake from his hands and send him crashing to the ground. Hell, even ripping his heart out would have been a trivial effort for me. But as I stood there looking at this human, I didn't want to hurt him. Because I had killed his mother. I deserved every bit of anger he was showing me.

I just wished he would put down his stake, because watching him brandish it at me was beginning to trigger an urge to punish him for his insolence.

"You are mistaken," I said, trying to keep my voice steady. "I never touched your mother."

"Don't lie to me," he snarled. "I'd recognize your face a mile away... the face of a cold-blooded killer... Do you remember the night you stormed our village?"

As he lifted the pendant inches away from my face, images of that bloody night flooded back. And then it happened. I lost control over my actions. It was as if I'd regressed to the same state I was in that horrific night, despite a part of me begging myself to stop.

I lunged at the human, knocking the wood from his hands and pinning him against the floor. I dug my claws deep into the sides of his neck until he screamed. He tried with all his might to throw me off, but he was helpless as a worm.

"How dare you," I hissed.

I was about to rip my fangs through his throat when two sharp thuds hit the base of my neck, sending spasms of pain down my spine. I turned in time to see two large ogres, iron clubs raised in the air, stained with blood.

My blood.

Chapter 11: Mona

I shuddered to think what might have happened had I arrived at The Tavern even a day later. It was my good luck that I'd met Saira in the pub that night and she'd warned me of our captain's plans. She'd said he wanted everyone on board the ship early the next day. We were to set sail in the evening, but there was preparation to be done.

She'd asked me dozens of questions about my time away, but to my annoyance, most of them had been centered around Kiev. She seemed to be determined to convince herself that I was secretly in love with him.

I'd only managed to sleep a few hours before I had to wake and make my way to our ship. But those hours in that clean soft bed, all alone, without the worry of devilish eyes watching me, had been heaven.

I was so relieved to be finally rid of the vampire, I didn't say goodbye. I couldn't deny the slight tinge of guilt I felt over it. Even in spite of everything, if it hadn't been for him carrying me on his back to the boat, I likely wouldn't have escaped Aviary.

But it wasn't difficult to brush thoughts of him away. What he had done was for his own survival, not mine. He had needed me and my boat. He hadn't done anything generous that made me owe him my thanks or farewell.

The only personal belongings I had were already strapped to my belt, so there was no packing to do. I left the room and walked down to the beach. I bathed in the sea before pulling on some clean clothes Michelle had given me.

Then I rounded up Evie and Kai, fastened them to my little boat and navigated it to where Saira had told me the main ship was anchored. I soon caught sight of it towering overhead. The ship was as I had remembered it and looked quite unscarred—Saira had told me that they'd left The Cove just in time before the hawks took over. It was made of dark brown wood, and at its stern and helm were carvings of dolphins. The sails were made of a deep orange fabric. *Leyla*, we called it—in memorial of the first dolphin that had ever served us.

In front of the stern, a group of two dozen dolphins were already gathering. Henry, one of our werewolf crew members, organized them into harnesses. Abandoning my boat, I led my own dolphins over to join the rest.

"Thanks, Mona," Henry called to me. "I'm glad you're safe."

I nodded and walked to the entrance of the boat. Members of the crew were already milling about, preparing everything for departure.

I headed straight to my room on the lowest level of the ship, avoiding speaking to anyone on the way. I arrived to find the door of my cabin slightly ajar. The captain sat on my cot. He encouraged me to call him by his first name, but most of the time I preferred to keep things formal—as I did with everyone—and addressed him as 'captain,' or Captain Matteo.

A smile spread across his handsome face as I entered.

"Saira told me you'd be joining us again," he said. "I'm very glad you're all right, Mona."

He placed a hand on my shoulder and squeezed it. I inched away, feeling uncomfortable. He knew I didn't like being touched, but I guessed his relief to see me safe again had made him forget that request of mine.

I smiled back faintly.

"Yes, I'm fine."

"How did you escape? Saira didn't tell me much…"

I really wasn't in the mood for recounting that wild escapade now. I just wanted to put it behind me and forget about it. But he would keep asking until I'd told him, so I gave him the briefest recap I could of what had happened.

"You were exceedingly lucky to have met that vampire," he said. "Kiev, you said his name was? Now, that's a funny coincidence! I met him on a walk along the beach just last night. Seemed to be an amiable fellow."

Eager to change the subject, I asked, "So how have things been with you? What happened? Saira filled me in on some things already. She told me you had to leave The Cove because of the hawks, but I didn't have much time to talk to her last night."

"Yes," he said, sighing. "They came suddenly and we had to act fast. You understand why we couldn't wait for your return."

"Of course," I said. "So what's the plan now?"

"We head back to our island," he replied. "And start planning our next attempt at getting our hands on a witch."

"What?" Heat rose in my body. "You can't seriously still be considering trying to storm The Sanct—"

"No, no. Not The Sanctuary," he said. I breathed out a sigh of relief. "Sorry, I forgot," he continued. "This is a development that happened while you were still in Aviary. The vampires of *The Black Bell* have three witches captive on their island. Each of them can wield magic."

I winced. I hardly needed that last piece of information; I'd never heard of any powerless witch other than myself.

I didn't need to ask him why he wanted the witches. It'd been a subject of discussion ever since we'd formed our crew. We suffered every day on our island not having adequate protection, constantly at risk of other pirates trying to plunder our resources. We'd had to build a large wall around the island, but even then, we needed guards to keep us safe. We could never all leave the island at once; even now, only half of us were on board the ship. The situation was distressing, especially for the vampires of our group, who were forced to live in underground tunnels during the daylight hours. The werewolves were lucky in that respect; they could be exposed to daylight at all hours, and at night, they'd have their transformation.

It was unfortunate that The Tavern had never been an option for us to make our home. Individuals were allowed to live there, but never groups as large as ours.

"But *The Black Bell*," I said, "You can't seriously be considering taking on that ship? Those vampires… It would be disastrous. They'd rip you all to shreds."

This entire subject was a painful reminder of my uselessness. I had no magic to help them when they needed it most.

"I agree," the captain said, nodding his head. "But you can understand why it's hard for us to just sit still knowing that *The Black Bell* contains three witches who would change our lives immeasurably. We only need one witch."

"How do you even plan to do this without getting yourselves killed?"

"We don't know yet." The captain rubbed his forehead. "We know they have an island, and the witches have cast upon it a protective spell of eternal night. I'm still discussing it with Saira and the others. I just thought you ought to know."

His face relaxed as he saw the look on my face. "Look, don't worry about this now. You've been through enough trauma. I'm sure you're still recovering and want time to yourself. We probably won't attempt to do anything for a few months anyway." He stood up and motioned to leave the room. "Oh, but speaking of news, our cook has been really honing his skills recently. He makes a marvellous seaweed dish. There's some left over from breakfast. If you head over to the kitchen I'm sure he'll be happy to oblige..."

"Thanks," I muttered, and Matteo left the room.

Now that he'd mentioned food, I couldn't deny that I was hungry. It had been too long since I'd eaten a cooked meal. I unstrapped my belt and placed it on my dressing table. I left my cabin and headed toward the kitchen.

I almost collided with Saira as she came dashing down the corridor.

"Mona," she panted. "Are you sure that vampire wasn't a friend?" In her human form, she was a short plump woman with bushy brown hair. Her grey eyes looked down at me with concern.

"Uh, yes," I said, looking at her with annoyance. Being old enough to be my mother, Saira would often try to look out for me as one. I knew she meant well, but I wished she would just leave me alone. There was a reason newcomers called her "Mother Wolf." She'd lost her only daughter and seemed to overcompensate by lavishing attention on others, regardless of whether or not it was wanted.

"All right," she said. "So then it won't mean anything to you that he's in the town square now about to be executed? Just thought you ought to know…"

Chapter 12: Kiev

Barely a month had passed since I'd met Natalie, and I was already wondering how I could have ever done without her in my life. I felt my chest tense up as she entered the moonlit meadow. God, she was beautiful. Sparkling eyes framed by perfectly arched brows. Thick dark hair flowing down to her thin waist. Soft red lips I craved every time I laid eyes on them.

Everything about her lit me up and made me ache with want.

She gave me a soft smile as our eyes met.

"Good evening, Kiev. You're on time, as always…"

It delighted me when she held out her hand, allowing me to kiss it. Placing her arm through mine, I led her through the meadow. She bent down every now and then to scoop up clusters of bright orange marigolds. Once she'd collected a fist full of them, she sat down in the grass.

"Sit here with me," she said, pointing to the space behind her.

I sat with my legs either side of her, her back against my chest. She dropped the flowers on the ground beside me. I ran my fingers through her hair until I'd separated it into small sections. One marigold at a time, I braided all the flowers into her hair. She ran her hands along my upper legs absentmindedly as I worked. I didn't let her get up until I'd finished. And once I had, she reached for my face and planted a tender kiss on my cheek.

I wanted to stay and relish her lips against my skin. Perhaps even return the gesture. But, as if my legs were no longer my own, I shot up and began running away in the opposite direction.

She called after me to stop.

But I couldn't.

My legs ran closer and closer toward a crater that had opened up at the end of the meadow. I reached the edge and gazed down at molten lava.

A wave of heat rushed up and burned my eyeballs.

"No!" Natalie shouted from behind me. "You don't have to do this, Kiev!"

Charred black hands shot out of the liquid, beckoning me to take the final step. Pebbles crumbled where my feet were planted and dropped into the lava.

It would be so easy to let myself fall. A few inches forward would be all it would take…

When I came to, the first sensation that hit me was agony coursing through my body. I couldn't open my eyes. They had deliberately placed me in direct contact with the sun. They had left nothing on me but a piece of cloth tied around my waist. I lay on my stomach on a hard wooden surface. I felt like a piece of meat being sizzled on a barbecue. I tried to move, but thick chains were attached to my ankles and wrists.

"This is what we do to anyone," a gruff voice said above me, "particularly newcomers, who think they can come here and act like they own the place."

A kick hit near my kidneys and I was sure that I was about to vomit. Rough hands gripped the back of my neck and pulled me to a standing position. My vision still a blur, I could just about make out crowds beneath me. I was standing on some kind of raised platform. I twisted my head to catch a glimpse of the person holding me. All I could make out was the outline of a large brown creature. An ogre. A soon as I turned to face him, he slapped my head back to position facing forward. Then I heard the sound of wood being sharpened behind me.

"I'm sure after this you'll all think twice next time you consider breaking the rules of The Tavern." The ogre chuckled beneath his breath. A few jeers echoed up from the crowds.

He let go of me and it was all I could to steady myself and not fall to the ground. I wasn't sure which would kill me first: the sun or the ogre.

"The Tavern is a place of peace and rest," the ogre continued. "You all know the rules! *This* is what happens to anyone who dares disrupt that."

Even though my eyelids felt like heavy weights, I somehow forced them to stay open and, in doing so, my vision slowly became clearer. The sea of faces was becoming more distinct and I could make out werewolves, ogres, and other creatures I couldn't put a name to. In the distance, beneath the shade of some trees, a few dozen vampires stood watching.

"This vampire here is guilty of attempted murder of a human… and this human here is guilty of attempted murder of a vampire."

A female scream pierced through the square.

"No! Please! Spare my husband!"

The sound of the ogre pulling on chains and someone choking

met my ears. I turned my head and saw the human who had attacked me. Like me, he had also been stripped of his clothes and wore nothing but a piece of cloth around his waist.

I was surprised to see the human there next to me on the platform. I wasn't used to such even-handed justice. As a vampire, I was used to humans always getting away with things and all blame being laid on vampires—and rightly so in the majority of cases.

"That vampire killed Jack's mother!" the female voice continued to scream out.

"Silence!" the ogre bellowed. "We are concerned only with events that take place within these walls."

"B-but… I'm bearing his child. Please! Have mercy!"

The ogre ignored her screams and turned his back against the crowds. I heard Jack's heavy breathing next to me. Each second that the ogre delayed my death was another second for the sun to continue roasting me alive. Part of me was hoping they'd kill me first to end my suffering. But it seemed that even that wish wouldn't be granted. One ogre slammed Jack down on the ground and held him still while the other picked up an axe, raising it in the air.

I closed my eyes as steel sliced flesh.

Chapter 13: Mona

I didn't know what to say. I clenched my fists and just stood there looking at Saira.

It wasn't my problem that he'd managed to get himself into trouble again. I couldn't keep carting him around places. I wasn't his mother. Or wife. Or even friend. He wasn't my responsibility. I'd taken him to The Tavern, one of the safest places existing in these parts, introduced him to Elizabeth, arranged for a roof over his head, and still he'd managed to wreck things in less than twelve hours after I'd left him. What more could I have done for the man? He probably deserved whatever punishment he was about to receive.

Don't even think about meddling, I told myself. *You remember how dangerous that is.*

"He's… not a friend. Like I said," I muttered.

Saira continued staring at me. I looked away, feeling awkward. Although I never had allowed myself to get close to her, she knew me better than I was comfortable with from our traveling together for years. We'd barely spent a month apart from each other since I'd left The Sanctuary.

She placed a hand on my shoulder. I stepped back, brushing her hand away.

"I used to be like you," she said quietly.

Her words aggravated me. *You have no idea what I am,* was what I wanted to spit out, but I held my tongue.

"Afraid," she said.

"I don't know what you're talking about," I said, the heat rising in my cheeks. "Afraid? Yes, maybe I am afraid of him. He could be a murderer for all I know."

Saira nodded and didn't say another word.

She turned around and left me standing there, staring after her.

Chapter 14: Kiev

The woman's screams intensified. She tried to break through the crowds, but another ogre caught hold of her and dragged her away from the scene.

The two ogres set their eyes on me. Chained by my hands and feet and severely weakened from the torment of the sun, I didn't attempt to fight. It would only make matters worse. One of them picked up a wooden stake while the other gripped hold of my neck and pressed me against a cool stone wall.

"Wait!" A voice boomed through the square. "I'll kill him instead."

I looked up and was confused to see a short round woman. As she made her way through the crowds with surprising speed, I realized that she was a werewolf. She leapt onto the platform, pushing the ogres aside. They both looked dumbstruck.

I racked my brains for any way I might have possibly harmed a werewolf, any reason why this complete stranger would want to kill me. Was this yet another person affected by my years of killing? Would I ever escape the scope of my bloody past? I was as confused as the ogres and audience watching.

"What?" one of the ogres grunted. "We have orders to execute him."

"In case you forget, I'm Saira, the great-granddaughter of Minneas. That alone should make you heed my words, ogre." She glared at him.

Saira. Mona's friend. I hadn't recognized her because I'd only seen her in her wolf form.

Nobody will have a chance to kill me if they don't hurry up. The sun will do the deed.

I was relieved when Saira stood over me and blocked the sun's direct contact with my skin. Without saying another word, she grabbed hold of the keys to the chains from the ogre's belt and unlocked me.

"Take my hand," she said to me under her breath.

I didn't think about what I was doing, or why I would trust her more than the ogres. If I refused the ogres would kill me. I grabbed her hand and she helped me to my feet, holding my waist to support me.

"But... where are you taking him?" the ogre shouted after us as Saira led me away from the platform.

"To a death far worse than what you would have inflicted on him."

Chapter 15: Kiev

"What are you doing?" I gasped as soon as we were out of sight of the square. I was relieved that she had led us over to some trees so my skin could gain some relief.

"There will be time for explanation later. For now, just hurry."

As we were approaching the beach, I decided to not press her and rather concentrate on walking faster—a task that was not at all easy when it felt like I was about to faint with exhaustion at any moment.

After what seemed like half an hour of walking on the hot sand, a large ship loomed in the distance. We ducked out of the trees lining the shore again and headed toward it. I let out a sigh of relief as Saira led me up the gangplank leading to the deck and entered a covering away from the direct sun.

As soon as we reached the shelter of the boat, my knees buckled.

Finally she answered my question. "Saving you," she said calmly.

I looked up at her face.

"Why?"

She hesitated, eyeing me. "I think you might prove to be a good asset for us. Just seemed a shame to have you go to waste. An errant vampire is quite a rare thing these days. Especially one as good-looking as you." She winked at me. "Most have already settled into their own groups, or indeed settled at The Tavern, and have no desire to move. They'll never know I didn't kill you in the end. Just make sure to never visit that place again, because if you do not only will you get in trouble, but I will too. I may be the great-granddaughter of one of the founding fathers of that island, but I can't pull rank on people there all that often when I'm not a resident. My rank was just enough to shock them into submission."

She frowned at me as I lay on the floor.

"First thing we need to do is get you cooled down. You look a complete wreck. You're no use to anyone in this state."

Every muscle and bone in my body ached as I forced myself into standing position. She walked me down some several staircases until we reached a lower mahogany deck and found a spare cabin. She let go of me and I dropped myself down on the bed.

"I'll ask for some spare clothes to be sent to you. For now, just lie down and get some sleep. Your body should recover on its own. Or did they apply any serum to you?"

I racked my brain for any memory of serum being applied to my body but found nothing.

"No idea," I said, shaking my head.

"Well, just sleep. We'll soon find out, in any case."

Saira left the room. I felt relieved to be alone in a safe bed. My body was overtaken with exhaustion and within a few minutes, I had fallen asleep.

Chapter 16: Mona

As we lifted the anchor and set sail, allowing the dolphins to begin pulling the ship into the open waters, I stood at the stern, watching the island fade away into the distance. The sun blazed down over the sparkling waters from its full height in the sky.

My thoughts drifted back to the vampire with red eyes. Another pang of guilt hit me. *It's not like you could have done anything, even if you had wanted to save him. He's under the jurisdiction of the Tavern's laws.*

Just forget about it.

I left the stern and walked past the dozens of people milling about on the deck, still organizing things for our journey. I wanted to retire to my room and lock myself up until tomorrow. I was still feeling run down from the days of lost sleep I'd had at Aviary thanks to being kept a slave there, at beck and call for Arron and his companions at all hours.

I'd done my fair share of work in getting the ship ready for sailing.

I trusted I wouldn't be needed for at least another few hours.

Since I'd chosen to be on the lowest level of the ship away from everyone, there were no windows in my room. Still, when I opened the door and found that it was dark, it surprised me because I didn't remember dimming my lantern before leaving.

But seeing as I was planning to get straight into bed and fall asleep, I didn't bother relighting it. I felt my way to my mattress, and lifted back the sheets.

I let out a scream.

I'd just attempted to sit on a cold body. A corpse, I was sure of it. But then, as if I wasn't already shaken enough, the corpse began to stir and blood-red eyes shot open in the darkness.

I ran out of the room, slamming the door behind me, screaming my lungs out.

"Saira!"

I blazed through the corridors, bellowing Saira's name. Some crew members hushed me, but I couldn't contain myself. The fright of finding that monster in my bed mixed with all the implications that now came with his presence on board caused me to lose control.

Saira came walking down a corridor toward me, her face quite expressionless.

"Why?" I panted, clutching her by the shoulders. "*Why?*"

"Why what?" she asked, an innocent expression on her face.

"Why is there a monster in my bed?"

"Oh, that. He was injured, dear. And he's a vampire. I needed somewhere dark and comfortable where he could recover. As you know, most of the rooms with beds on this ship have windows."

"Why couldn't you take him to one of the other rooms below deck? Or hell, I don't know, just draw the blinds of one of the rooms in the upper deck!"

Saira shook her head. "All the other bedrooms were occupied at the time. And I was panicking. I just needed to get him somewhere dark and safe as soon as possible. He was in a dreadful state when I found him. I'm sorry, Mona. I didn't know it would upset you so much…"

"Why did you save him and bring him here?" I spluttered. "I told you already, he's *not* my friend!"

"My decision to save him had nothing to do with you, contrary to what you might think. As a founding member of this crew, I have a right to recruit others." She glared at me. "And I thought leaving him to be killed would be a waste of a perfectly capable crew member."

Her answers infuriated me. She was lying to my face. She had done this deliberately to throw the vampire in my way. Having lost a daughter made her do the most erratic things.

"And now what?" I hissed. "I need my room back!"

"You'll get it back," she said. "Just give him a few more hours of rest to let his body finish healing. Then I'll remove him and put him up in another room. Okay?"

The situation couldn't have been further from okay. But she sped off before I had a chance to protest again. By now, a group of new crew members—both vampires and werewolves—were listening in from a distance. Hating to be the center of attention, I hurried away from them.

I found myself walking back toward my cabin. When I reached the door, I placed my ear against it, hoping to hear that he had woken up. But from the gentle breathing, he had fallen asleep again.

Comforted that at least he wouldn't be staring at me again through the darkness, I dared open the door. I fumbled for the lantern and turned it on. He still didn't stir.

I stepped toward the bed and hovered over him, examining his

A SHADE OF KIEV

face and body. I didn't notice any injuries. His skin looked totally smooth. I didn't understand why he had to sleep more, least of all in my bed.

I sat down in the chair a few feet away and continued glaring at him.

Watching Kiev sleeping on my bed was starting to make me feel sleepy. I wished he would wake up and leave so I could have my bed back. *Now I'll have to make a trip to the laundry room and change the sheets*, I reminded myself, scowling.

Despite myself, my breath hitched a little as he stirred on the mattress, causing the sheet to slide off him and reveal more of his almost naked form. He had fabric wrapped around his waist, but otherwise the people of The Tavern had stripped him bare. There wasn't a part of his toned body that didn't exude strength.

Why is this happening?

And why the hell did I have to ask him those stupid questions?

Now that he had been officially recruited by Saira as a crew member, worry filled me as I thought of the worst-case scenario: I might never see the back of him. I might forever be plagued with his presence. Unless I abandoned my crew, which I couldn't do easily.

My skin tingled as I watched him sleep.

And I felt nervous.

More nervous than I had in years.

Chapter 17: Kiev

As I lay in bed, the old oak door to my room creaked open.

Clara, the woman my Elder forced me to call sister, appeared in the doorway. She wore nothing but thin silk lingerie.

"Get up," she hissed. "Did I give you permission to sleep at this time?"

Unwilling to acknowledge her presence, I let my exhausted body remain still on the mattress. The bed shook as she climbed onto it. Cold hands closed around my ankles as she pulled at my legs. I held on to the headboard and kicked her away. I should have known that would only infuriate her further.

"I called you to my bed an hour ago. Why are you still here?"

She climbed onto my back and tore off my nightshirt with her claws, ripping my skin in the process. I winced as her lips pressed against the back of my neck, her legs spread out on either side of my waist.

Then came the lashes. Brandishing a whip, she cut into my flesh until blood soaked the sheets.

"Father gave you to me for a hundred years. Barely twenty have

passed. It's time you stopped fighting me, Kiev…"

I woke to see Mona sitting at the opposite end of the room. She looked daggers at me.

"Is… Is this your cabin?" I rubbed my eyes, attempting to brush away any memory of the nightmare I'd just had.

"Yes." The tone of her voice was traced with irritation, yet she was attempting to keep her face expressionless. She stood up, handing me a set of fresh clothes. "These were brought for you. You probably want to wear them now." Her eyes roamed the length of my body. "You should leave."

I took them from her and pulled them on. No sooner had I pulled the shirt on than she opened the cabin door.

"Where should I go?"

"Ask Saira."

I stepped out of the cabin. She slammed the door behind me.

I walked along the corridor toward a door that led to the stairs I had climbed down with Saira. I pushed it open and ascended the stairs, looking around as I did. A few vampires and werewolves bustled about on the second deck, but it was quieter now than when I had first arrived.

I approached a female vampire carrying a large bundle of sheets and asked, "Where can I find Saira?"

She eyed me, then smiled coyly, brushing a few strands of dark hair behind her ear. "You're new here, aren't you?" she said.

I nodded.

"I suggest going to the captain's room and asking there. He might have seen her. You never know, she could be with him."

"Where's the captain's room?" I asked.

"Walk to the end of this hallway"—she gestured with her hand—

"then take the first left and it's the last cabin at the end of that corridor."

I nodded and motioned to leave. She brushed a hand against my shoulder, her lips still curved in a smile. "And, in case you were interested," she whispered, "my name is Lorena. My cabin isn't far from the captain's, just a couple of doors along to the right."

She was attractive. But I wasn't in the mood for playing around. I brushed her hand away and walked away.

I realized that I knew nothing about the captain at all—whether he was a werewolf, vampire, or perhaps another species entirely. I followed her directions and once I reached the end of the corridor, I paused and placed my ear to the door. I could hear a soft shuffling of papers. I rapped on the door three times and waited.

Footsteps sounded and the door swung open.

My heart skipped a beat.

In the doorway stood the man I'd met on the beach.

Matteo Borgia.

I took a step back involuntarily.

"You're... you're the captain of this ship?"

The man smiled.

"Yes."

He opened the door wider and gestured for me to step inside. I found myself rooted to the spot. He held out his hand. I shook it after a pause. I looked around his cabin, nervous. The room was lined with shelves filled with books, and maps covered the wooden walls. There was a large window fixed to the side of the wall, though the blinds were drawn to keep the sun out.

He wore a freshly starched white shirt rolled up to his elbows and black shorts that stretched down below his knees. I wanted to walk right out of his cabin—hell, jump off the ship. Suddenly, being back in that town square seemed more appealing than being on the same boat as Natalie's brother. Each time he looked my way, daggers of guilt pierced through me.

Now that I'd come face to face with him again, the resemblance really was unmistakable. I saw Natalie in his eyes, and to think he might have not found out about his own sister's death due to being in a different realm made me feel sick to my stomach.

"Take a seat, Kiev. Make yourself comfortable. And welcome aboard. Saira did mention to me in passing that you have become the newest member of our crew. And what a surprise it was! I certainly hadn't been expecting to see you again."

I gulped and took a seat opposite his mahogany desk.

"Are you thirsty?" He indicated a jug of blood that was perched on a shelf. I could already smell that it was fish blood. I had been thirsty a few moments before stepping into his office. Now, all thirst had vanished.

I shook my head.

He poured a glass for himself and sat down behind his desk.

"What can I do for you?"

"I… I'm looking for Saira."

"Why do you need her?"

"She put me up in the wrong room."

"Saira is busy now. But if you need a new room I'm sure that I can assist."

He finished his blood, then got up and opened one of his desk drawers, pulled out a ring of keys and walked toward the door. He opened the door and courteously stepped aside, letting me step out first. I obliged and once we were walking down the corridor toward—I wasn't even sure where—he began speaking again.

"Saira told me about the incident in the town square. Narrow escape, huh?"

My stomach formed in knots.

"Yes…"

"What got you into so much trouble?" He asked the question casually but I could detect a hint of curiosity in his voice, perhaps even mistrust.

"A man attacked me in the bar. I retaliated in self defense."

"I see." He nodded. "Yes. Violence against another inhabitant is the most serious form of crime on that island. It doesn't matter how it was instigated. Some people see the rule as foolish and unfair, whereas others recognize that it's required. You get all sorts passing through that place. They have to rule the inhabitants with an iron fist or else it would be chaos and the purpose of the island would be defeated."

We continued walking down the corridor and once we reached the end, he opened a door and led us down to the level below. We stopped outside a door. He unlocked it and walked inside, drawing the blinds to block out the sun. It was a decent-sized cabin—larger than Mona's—with a small shower room en suite.

I turned to Matteo and said "Thank you," hoping that he'd now turn around and leave.

He placed some keys on the small dressing table and said, "Once again, nice to see you, Kiev. I'll tell Saira to come down and find you once she's finished her tasks."

He beamed another smile at me before backing out of the room and closing the door behind him.

Chapter 18: Kiev

I lay in bed and looked up at the ceiling. I couldn't stop thinking about Matteo. I wondered how long I might end up staying on that ship. As he was the captain—the most prominent member aboard—it wasn't like I could easily hide from or avoid him. Being forced to face him each day, memories of that bloody night resurfacing in my mind each time our eyes met, was something I wasn't sure I could handle.

But I had no alternative. At least for now.

Hours passed as I lost myself in thought. I lifted the blinds and realized that night had fallen. Thunder rolled overhead and rain pattered against the glass. As I got up to leave the cabin to stretch my legs, the deafening ringing of a bell echoed from outside. The boat shuddered so violently that I almost lost balance. The lantern in my cabin swung off its hook and smashed on the ground, splinters of glass sent digging into my ankles. I reached the window and looked out. The thick rain made it impossible for me to see far.

The ringing faded away into the distance and once the rocking stopped, I stepped out of my room. A dozen others had done the same, including a werewolf in the cabin next to mine.

"What was that?" I asked.

His eyes were wide with alarm.

"*The Black Bell*," he whispered back.

"What?"

Ignoring my question, he dashed down the corridor. Everyone around me shared the same look of fear. I followed the direction he was heading in, toward the upper deck.

When I arrived, crowds of vampires and werewolves had gathered in the rain, most of them standing at the stern, looking out at the ocean. I spotted Saira crouching down on the floor near the helm. She looked up at me as I approached.

"What happened?" I asked.

"We had to, uh, change course."

"Why?"

"To avoid *The Black Bell*." She spoke as though I should understand what on earth she was talking about. When she saw me looking at her blankly, she continued, "It's a ship of pirates the likes of which you don't ever want to find yourself colliding with. We didn't notice them coming in this weather. The dolphins had to swerve quickly."

"What kind of pirates?"

"They're vampires. But everything is under control now. You can go back down to your room with everyone else."

Her words sent curiosity burning through me. I wanted to ask her more about these vampires. I wondered if I had ever met them during my time with the Elders. But she didn't give me a chance. As soon as she'd spoken the last sentence she hurried away. I scanned the deck for anyone else I could approach about the incident, but the crowds were now dispersing, everyone returning back to their rooms for the night.

I walked over to the edge of the deck and, holding onto the railing, gazed out at the dark ocean. Still failing to see signs of any distant ship, I prowled around on the deck for a while longer before descending again to the lower levels. I'd return to my cabin and attempt to gain more information the next day.

However, once I'd reached my level, I caught sight of Mona walking barefoot toward me. She wore a thin nightdress that fell just above her knees. As soon as she caught sight of me, she did a one-eighty and began walking full speed in the opposite direction.

"Wait," I called.

Mona started to run. I hurried forward until I'd caught up with her. I stood in front of her, blocking her way so she had no choice but to stop.

"What?" She kept her eyes on the wooden floorboards.

"What do you know about *The Black Bell*?"

"Why?" she muttered.

"I just want to know." We were only a few doors away from my cabin. I caught hold of her hand and pulled her toward my door.

"Don't touch me!"

Ignoring her, I pushed her down into a chair, closed the door and then took a seat on my bed. I guessed that if she was sitting down rather than standing in the corridor outside she'd give me a fuller answer. I looked at her expectantly.

"So, tell me."

"Why should I?" she spat.

"Because I asked you to," I growled. Her refusal to obey me was beginning to make me question her safety around me again.

"I owe you nothing, vampire." Sitting forward in her chair, she looked at me defiantly. "You've picked the wrong girl to try to intimidate."

She stood up and slapped me across the face. Then she exited my cabin, slamming the door behind her with such force that the floor shook.

I felt stunned that she would have dared even attempt such a thing, much less do it. My entire body trembled to chase her down. I wanted to punish her, maim her for her insolence. I wanted to see her suffer. But somehow, I found within me the strength to remain still as her footsteps disappeared down the corridor.

It felt like another blackout might take hold of me and I would have no choice but to run after her. If that happened, I would end her life. I tried to take deep breaths. I lay back on the bed and gripped the sheets, closing my eyes.

I opened them again only after a few hours, once my rage had subsided and my mind was cool enough to have coherent thoughts. I played the scene that had just passed over in my head. In the heat of her presence, I'd only been capable of seeing faults in her behavior. I'd only been able to see her disobedience to my will.

But now that she was gone, the sickness of my own actions hit me full force.

Her slap had shaken something in me.

Why did I feel so much rage?

What right do I have to demand anything of her?

Is this really the man I want to be?

Chapter 19: Mona

We arrived back at our island the following evening. Since we'd returned earlier than expected and the sun was still setting, the vampires used the straw umbrellas we kept on the ship at all times to avoid getting struck by the sun.

Once I'd scanned the beach for Kiev, I let the crowd walk up ahead of me, trailing behind. We walked along the outskirts of the wall we'd built around the island for about a quarter of a mile until we reached the large iron gate that served as our entrance.

Matteo knocked. It creaked open after several minutes. I was the last to enter and was greeted by Brett, our resident ogre. Brett and I were the only residents of the island who weren't vampires or werewolves.

"All right, Mona?" He smiled warmly, wrinkles forming in his dark leathery skin around his eyes. "Good to see you all back safely."

He locked the gate behind me. "Has there been a lot of trouble since we left?" I asked.

"Just the usual. We had some more attempted break-ins. But we managed to head them off."

I sighed, though at least things hadn't gotten worse since we'd been away.

Apparently, before us, the island had never been occupied before. We'd been told it was because it was too dangerous, being right at the juncture of the islands that made up Triquetra—an area renowned for the most notorious of pirates. But we'd taken the chance because even this seemed better than the fate we'd been heading for with all of us crammed together on the ship.

I walked away from the gate and entered the circular clearing just before the entrance to the woods. Still careful to stray behind the others, I made my way along the dirt path. After about a mile, the vampires parted from the werewolves. They all descended into the entrance of an underground tunnel.

Although the island was thick with broad-leaved trees, the shade they provided wasn't sufficient for the vampires to live comfortably above ground. They needed somewhere cooler and darker to live. We'd had to carve out caves underground for them to stay in during the day, while the werewolves kept watch. At night, the vampires could move easily around the island, and it was their turn to guard.

Soon after the vampires had strayed away from the path, the werewolves up ahead were greeted by another group of werewolves who'd stayed back from our trip to The Cove to take care of the island. They emerged from the shade of the trees, some calling out the names of loved ones and embracing. We walked through the forest until we reached another clearing at the center of the island. Just a few meters away was a lake. It was surrounding this lake that the werewolves had made their homes. When we'd first arrived they'd decided it was best for their homes to be built up in the trees.

Having wild animals on the island was both a blessing and a curse; without them, we wouldn't have had as much choice of food, yet they also proved to be a great annoyance.

As for myself, I'd wanted to be more isolated from the rest of them. I recognized that I couldn't have my home on the ground either. I'd debated for a while about having my home up in the trees along with the werewolves, and I'd even tried it at one point. But I found the atmosphere too stifling. I needed my own space. Saira and Matteo had granted my request and helped build a wooden house on stilts right in the middle of the lake. It consisted only of one room—containing a bed, a cooking area, a table and a chair—and a bathroom. I enjoyed the solitude it gave me. And being in the center of the island, surrounded by creatures much stronger than me, I felt safe.

Once a day I visited the mainland to fill up my water bucket from the well, because I didn't like the taste of water stored in my cabin for more than a day. But other than that, my home was self-sustaining. The fish and water plants I found in the lake were all I needed for food.

Moving away from the crowd before Saira spotted me, I walked down to the bank of the lake. I was relieved to see my old rowing boat where I had left it. I had insisted that there only be one boat kept in the lake—mine. This ensured that nobody ever disturbed me unless it was about something important, because they had to get wet in order to reach me.

I climbed into the boat, grabbed hold of the oars and began rowing. I was itching to feel the covers of my bed around me again. To relish the silence that my lake house afforded me. If it weren't for it, I would have gone mad long ago. I didn't know how I had managed to survive until we found the island. Living on the ship full-time and being surrounded by crowds of creatures all milling about in such a small space... The island truly had been a Godsend. And not just for me. For all of us. The vampires and werewolves used to be tripping over themselves. And while that still happened, inevitably, it was a rarer occurrence.

As I neared the center of the lake, my little cabin came into view. The red wood near the roof had developed an excess of moss, but that was nothing that some scrubbing wouldn't fix. Each of the five large windows would also need washing. I smiled when I saw that the blue lilies I had planted around the stilts supporting the cabin had multiplied and were now in full bloom. Overall, I was relieved to see that my home appeared in no worse a state than I had left it in.

I climbed out of the boat and onto the small wooden platform leading to my front door. Before going inside, I took a moment to look around at the calm waters. The beauty and serenity of the lake never failed to take my breath away.

It felt like being on my own island. An island within an island.

But, even with these surroundings, I couldn't say that my life was happy. Or fulfilling.

It was merely survivable.

Chapter 20: Kiev

As the sun set, I followed the group of vampires into a circular hole that had been dug into the forest's undergrowth. It resembled the gaping entrance of a cave. There wasn't even a door.

My opinion of the vampires' accommodations didn't improve on entering. We walked into a cavern that split off into various dark passageways. The walls, ceilings, and ground were made of dirt. Unsurprisingly, the whole place smelled of damp soil.

I followed a few vampires down one of the passageways. Lanterns lined the walls at intervals, which confused me because as vampires we didn't need them. I supposed that it was just to add a touch of civilization, so we wouldn't feel like animals living in this burrow.

As I walked down the corridor, I peeked into the rooms whose doors were open. Rooms was a generous description. They were almost entirely bare—and of course windowless—except for thin straw mattresses on the ground and a few personal belongings.

I wondered to myself whether the werewolves' residences were any better. Somehow, I doubted it. The accommodations here were a far cry from what I'd grown accustomed to over the centuries. Still, as long as I had a room to myself, I wasn't about to complain.

I didn't know where Saira had gone, and I had no idea which room was to be mine. I walked around the passageways for a while, looking for someone to approach. I caught sight of Lorena, the attractive female vampire I'd asked for directions from back on the ship. I'd already guessed what her answer to my question would be before I had asked it.

"Didn't Saira tell you she meant for you to share my room?"

I looked at her, unamused. She chuckled at her own joke before saying in a more serious tone, "I don't know. I'm surprised she didn't already assign you one. You should ask the captain. I can show you his room, if you want?"

I shook my head. I didn't want to have to seek him out for anything if I could possibly avoid it.

"No, I'll figure it out," I said.

I continued walking along the passageways. Eventually, I found myself alone. I decided my best option was to seek out Saira. I made my way back to the central area of the tunnels and climbed the slope leading out into the night's fresh air.

I didn't have to walk long before a wolf came bounding toward me.

"Sorry, Kiev," Saira panted. "I became occupied with other matters."

"I need to know which room I should be stay—"

"Yes, yes. I know. But before I get you settled down, I need to discuss something with you. Care to take a walk?" She gestured toward the forest with her paw.

"I suppose so," I said.

It felt odd walking alongside her during her transformation. Her walking on four paws meant I was constantly having to talk down at her.

She led me away from the tunnels and deeper into the forest. I took in the atmosphere as we walked in silence beneath the towering trees. Now that it was dark, I realized how much this place reminded me of The Shade. *Sofia's island*. A wave of nostalgia flooded over me. The snaking pathways, the tree houses, the distant lulling of the waves against the shore… everything brought back memories of the visits I'd made to that magnificent island. Although, of course, The Shade's lavish penthouses and other obscene luxuries were nonexistent here. Still, in the early years of The Shade's development, the Novak clan hadn't started out with much more to work with than what was currently here on this island.

"What do you call this place?" I found myself asking.

"What do you mean?"

"Doesn't this island have a name?"

She shook her head. "We haven't come up with a name for it. We normally just refer to it as *our island*… but on to more important matters. I need to discuss what your service is to be while you're staying here with us."

I raised a brow at her.

"Yes," she said, "we do have the same system as The Tavern. If you stay with us in our community, then you must contribute."

"Continue," I muttered.

"The time of most vampires and werewolves is spent on guard duty around the walls of this island. They keep watch and alert the rest of us if any pirates are spotted within a five-mile radius."

"And how many hours—"

"You, on the other hand," she interrupted, "will have a different duty from the rest of us." She stopped walking and looked up at me. "But before I reveal it to you, you must promise me that you won't tell anybody about this. Not a soul. Not even Matteo. Do you promise?"

I frowned at her. "What are you—"

"And you must understand that if you break this promise, I'll have you thrown off of this island."

I didn't know what to make of this wolf. The mild demeanor she'd assumed around me up until now completely contradicted the words that came out of her mouth.

"Excuse me? Who are *you* to issue commands to me, anyway? You're not even the captain of this—"

"Oh, yes. Everyone calls Matteo the captain," the wolf chuckled. "But Matteo and I rule over this place jointly. In fact, I have more influence than him over who gets what task on this island."

She watched me for my reaction. I stared down at her, furious at how helpless I was. She had me in a corner, and there was nothing I could do about it.

I nodded reluctantly.

"What's that?" she asked as though she were speaking to a child. "Is that you agreeing, son? You need to spell it out for old Saira, dear, so I'm sure I'm not just imagining things. Do you promise not to tell a soul?"

"Yes," I muttered.

"Yes, what?"

"I promise."

"Ah, good." Her mouth split into a grin. "So, your task is to become Mona's friend."

My jaw dropped.

"What?"

"Oh, your hearing is quite adequate." She smiled up at me. "I'm sure you heard."

"Are you insane?"

She laughed. "Well, that's really beside the point, isn't it?"

I struggled to find words to express my disbelief.

"I have no idea what you're asking of me," I concluded.

"What don't you understand about it? I'm sure I worded it quite—"

The wolf's way of answering questions while providing no answers at all exasperated me. "Why the hell do you want me to become Mona's friend?" I asked, my voice growing louder with each word I spoke.

"You don't need to know that. You just need to obey. And hush," she whispered, knocking her paw against my leg. "You promised to keep quiet about this."

I inhaled deeply, calling on the crisp night air to calm my flaring temper.

"So is this why you rescued me?" I asked.

"Not necessarily," she replied.

"What's that supposed to mean?" I spat.

"I'm not saying becoming Mona's friend will always be the only task you're assigned while you're on this island. Once you become her friend, it's more than likely that I'll assign you a new task."

I grabbed a branch and ripped it from its trunk, snapping it over my leg in frustration.

Calm down. You can't afford to lose it with this wolf.

"What does becoming her friend even mean?"

"Well, right now she insists that you are not her friend," Saira said. "So we need to have the opposite situation."

"Which means?" I asked through gritted teeth.

"Spend time with her. Make her want to spend time with you. Make her happy. Make her like you. And look out for her."

Her last words almost sent me over the edge. I had to pause for a few moments in an attempt to rein myself in.

"Look at me," I said, my voice murderously low. "Is this the face of a babysitter?"

Saira smiled again. That placid, patronizing smile. "I didn't say I wanted you to babysit her," she said. "Looking after her is just part of your friendship."

"But she hates me!" I hissed. "What makes you think she'd ever want me to befriend her?"

"Ah," Saira said, winking at me. "That's where your magic comes in. You need to win her over with your charms."

"I have no charms," I seethed.

"All men have charms. Some just choose to ignore them."

"And what if I fail?"

"You'll have to leave. Sorry, dear. There has to be something at stake here or you may not put in your full effort."

"And if by some miracle I succeed?" I scowled.

"Next time I ask Mona if you are her friend, she will say yes. After that, I promise you can have some other duty, like guarding the wall at night."

Seeing me still pacing up and down, she sighed and said, "Look, you're a good-looking fellow. You'll manage. Relax. Just be yourself."

Be yourself.

I smiled bitterly at the notion.

"And just remember: if Mona, Matteo, or anyone else finds out that you are becoming her friend because of an order, you'll be off this island before you can say Saira."

Chapter 21: Kiev

Saira led me deeper into the woods until we reached the banks of a lake. She indicated a small lake house in the center and informed me that this was Mona's home. And after that, she refused to say another word to me. She turned away and sprinted back toward the tunnels, forcing me to chase after her. I asked further questions of her as we ran, but she ignored them all.

On arriving outside the dirt hole that was now to be my home, I followed her inside. She led me along a passageway and stopped outside a door. She pushed it open and gestured for me to enter.

This room was no different to any of the other rooms I had seen earlier in this place. As I sat down on the mattress, Saira pushed the door closed and scampered away.

I still had not even the faintest clue why the wolf had given me this senseless task. Why did Mona even need my friendship? Surely there were plenty of other creatures on this island she'd known longer than me, who would be better candidates if Saira really was insistent on her having company.

Mona had already admitted to me that she liked being alone. Why would Saira want to make her miserable by forcing her to be around people?

A part of me was still in denial, half believing that I'd wake up tomorrow to realize that this had all been some kind of crazy dream. The truth was, my mind simply had no idea how to even start wrapping my mind around the task. I wasn't capable of friendship. And with that witch, of all people? I grimaced as I recalled my last encounter with her.

I haven't exactly made things any easier for myself.

I felt stifled by the room. The walls felt too close. I left to take another walk into the night, this time alone. I walked through the forest until I reached the large wall that surrounded the island. I walked next to it, following it wherever it took me around the small island, past woods, lakes, hills, until finally the wall melted into the base of a rocky black mountain.

I looked up to gauge its height. I could reach the top by leaping, but my limbs were hungry for the challenge of the climb. Gripping hold of some rocks at its base, I began my ascent. I didn't stop until I reached its peak. Hoisting myself up onto the grassy plateau, I realized that I was not alone.

A group of four vampires sat in a corner, their backs facing me as they dangled their legs off the cliff, looking out at the ocean. It was only after taking a better look that I realized one of those vampires was Matteo. I considered jumping back down again before anyone noticed me, but it was too late.

"Kiev."

Matteo had turned toward me, a look of surprise in his eyes. He smiled and beckoned me over. Once I'd reached him, he stood up and, placing a hand on my shoulder, said, "I've been meaning to talk to you."

He led me to a quiet corner away from the others and turned again toward the ocean.

"This is our best vantage point," he said.

I could very well believe that. The view was breathtaking. I could see for miles in all directions around the island.

"And it's here that I would like you to come to serve your duty as guard."

I looked at him, not sure how to break the news to him that Saira had already appointed me to a duty. I couldn't tell him what my task was, but she didn't tell me I couldn't say that I *had* a task.

"Saira has given me work," I said.

He raised a brow.

"Oh? What's that?"

"She forbade me to tell you."

"Very well." He smiled knowingly and nodded. "Sounds like Saira. I won't interfere."

Please do interfere, I thought. I would have happily offered to guard the place for twice my fair share of time if it meant freeing myself from what Saira had in store for me. I had half a mind to request this of him. But the idea of asking favors from him was too uncomfortable for me to entertain.

"Did Saira already go through the rules of this island with you?" he asked.

I shook my head.

"Well, then I had better do so now. We don't want you getting into any more sticky situations." He smiled, eyeing me. "Don't worry—we're not as strict as The Tavern. That doesn't mean you can take our guidelines lightly, mind you. We'd have anarchy otherwise."

"I understand," I said.

"Good. Our rules are actually similar to The Tavern's. But self-defense is not a crime here. Deliberate unprovoked violence, however, is punishable by permanent expulsion. Stealing from any of us will also have you expelled. As for contributing to our community, normally you would take your turn at night duty, though it seems that Saira already has you occupied with other things. Other than this, you will take part in whatever missions or expeditions we undertake." He turned his eyes toward me.

I nodded.

"Sounds simple enough." I looked back out toward the ocean. "What are they?" I couldn't keep myself from asking, seeing the silhouettes of dozens of islands in the distance.

"Our neighbors," he said with a grimace. "All pirates. This whole area is notorious. That's why we can never afford to be lax on security."

"Do you have many attacks?"

"Oh, yes. Sometimes on a weekly basis. There are often new pirates passing through these waters who are willing to try their hand at stealing some unearned goods." He pointed downward. The remains of seven bodies hung skewered on pikes—apparently ogres. "That's what we do to those who try to plunder us."

There was an uncomfortable pause as I watched the skeletons swaying in the wind.

"Well, if that's all, captain, I think I'll head off."

"Good luck," he said, grinning.

I turned away and rushed down the mountain. I continued my tour around the island, occasionally passing a thick snake slithering in the undergrowth, or a deer-like animal with twisted horns I couldn't quite put a name to.

As each hour passed, I felt worse and worse about my assignment. I didn't know how I would be able to spring from where I'd left off with Mona into having her accept me as a friend. My ego twinged at the thought of apologizing for my behavior, even though I did regret the way I had handled the situation.

I hated the idea of chasing after her. I wasn't used to jumping through hoops. Not for anyone, other than my father.

Worst of all, I still didn't have control over my blackouts. If she aggravated me again, I felt nervous as to how I might react. I had managed to contain myself back on the ship, but it had been a struggle I had no desire to repeat.

Eventually as the sky began to lighten, a warm orange glow appearing along the horizon, I returned to my room in the tunnels. Sitting down on the old mattress, I leaned my back against the wall and stretched out my legs.

I didn't leave my room for the entire day. I just sat there, looking at the dirt walls and steeling myself for what was to come. Complaining and protesting were pointless. This was the first task that Saira had given me and—as much as I detested the control she had over me—if I didn't complete it, she would have me thrown off of the island. I would be cast adrift and would surely perish in the ocean.

Maybe I would find an alternative place to stay in the coming weeks, but I had nothing of the sort yet.

My best course of action was to swallow my pride and get this madness over with as soon as possible. After that, Saira would assign me to guard the island like the rest of the vampires. The job I should have had to start with.

A knocking at my door broke through my thoughts.

"Enter," I called.

A large ogre swung the door open. On seeing me, he smiled and held out an oversized hand. I stood up and shook it.

"I'm Brett," he said, his mustard-yellow eyes lighting up. "I'm doing some roasting up on the hill nearby. There will be blood, too. Since you're new, I thought you might welcome the chance to meet some of us."

I had no desire to meet anybody. But, realizing that I was in need of blood, I nodded and followed him out of the tunnels. He led me to the top of a high grassy hill nearby where a bonfire had been lit. A crowd of vampires and werewolves—none of whom I recognized— sat around it, drinking and talking.

Brett grabbed a jug of blood from near the fire and poured some into a clay cup. I sniffed it. This was neither fish nor snake blood. It was that of some kind of four-legged mammal—perhaps one of the deer I'd seen earlier. It was still unsatisfying compared to human blood, but its flavor was at least less revolting to me than the former two.

I sat in the shadows, away from the group, and drank from my cup. My eyes glazed over as the bonfire's flames licked the warm night air. My mind drifted back to thoughts of Mona. I started racking my brain for ideas as to what my first move should be, trying to form a strategy. My first hurdle would be meeting her face to face. If she rarely came out of her lake house, I would have to swim across the lake just to stand in front of her.

Lost in my thoughts and speculations, I didn't notice a slim figure approach the clearing. It was only after several minutes that I looked up and saw the witch standing on the other side of the bonfire. A blond vampire was by her side—the same one who'd first approached me on the beach back at The Tavern. I realized my first opportunity had come sooner than I had expected.

I smirked.

This might just be an easy win…

Chapter 22: Mona

It was that time of night when I needed fresh water.

After the short boat ride to the mainland, I began my walk through the werewolves' residential area toward the other side of the forest. I passed the armory along the way—a small chamber underground where we kept all of the valuable tools and weapons that we had acquired throughout the years, mainly through plundering other pirates at sea.

After about an hour, I arrived at the small hole in the ground. Attaching my bucket to a rope, I lowered it into the well, trying to make as little noise as possible. As I pulled it back up, sudden laughter sounded out in the distance, coming from the direction of the nearby hill. I looked up to see the flickering of a fire.

The light breeze carried a delicious smell toward me. I salivated. Momentarily distracted, I lost my grip on the rope and the bucket clattered to the bottom of the well.

A few seconds later, a gruff voice called out.

"Hey!"

I didn't need to see though the dark to know that it was Brett. An imposing figure stood up and walked down the hill toward me. His face broke out into a big smile.

"Mona! I'm just cooking something up there. You hungry?"

I was famished. It would be at least an hour before I'd have a meal of my own ready. The smell of hot food was almost too much to bear. Despite my better judgment, I nodded.

I followed him up the hill, but on reaching the top immediately regretted my decision. A dozen vampires sat in the circle around the fire, and there were also some werewolves who had not yet gone to bed.

Worried about spotting a certain red-eyed vampire, I averted my eyes to the ground and followed Brett around the circle, trying to hide behind him. I sat down on the grass next to the ogre. He reached into the fire and pulled out a colorful skewer of roasted sea plants. I would have bitten into them instantly had they not been piping hot.

"Well, I'm off to bed now," Brett muttered, standing up.

"Oh?"

Now that Brett's large form had moved, I was in full view of the group.

"Yeah. I'm sorry, Mona. I'm exhausted. I'll see you around..."

The ogre plodded away. I turned my back on the crowd to face the ocean. But it seemed that I hadn't escaped attention.

I felt a tap on my shoulder.

On turning around, I groaned.

Giles.

The blond vampire towered over me, one hand hidden behind his back. Apart from Kiev, he was our newest vampire recruit. He'd been with us for over five months, but it seemed that he still hadn't learned his lesson when it came to badgering me.

"How are you, Mona?" I smelt the rum on his breath as soon as he opened his mouth. "I've missed you."

I ignored him and stood up.

"I've b-brought you something." He withdrew a shiny conch shell from behind his back. "Do you like it? I found it myself."

His grey eyes were bloodshot and rolled in their sockets. I'd never seen him so drunk. His presence unnerved me. I turned to walk away, still without saying a word, but his hand reached out and latched onto my arm.

"Don't you like it?"

Normally, his advances were irritating, or awkward at best. But this night was different. I scoured the crowd more closely for the first time, hoping I might see Matteo or Saira sitting there. That was when I caught sight of red eyes glinting at me from the shadows.

I looked back at Giles.

"Let go, Giles," I hissed.

With my free hand, I reached for the dagger I kept strapped to my belt. But, dropping the shell, he caught that hand too. Despite him being intoxicated, it frightened me how fast his reflexes were.

"And if I don't leave you alone?" he whispered, a grin forming on his lips.

The vampire's grip tightened. When I looked around again, everyone seemed too busy merrymaking to notice my predicament. Except Kiev, who sat alone. He held my gaze with his dark crimson eyes.

Then he stood up, and in what felt like less than two seconds, he had reached us. He placed a hand on Giles' shoulder and—to my shock—said in a low menacing voice, "Don't touch her."

Giles swiveled his neck around, blinking at Kiev.

"And who are you? Her uncle?" He chuckled.

Kiev's glare didn't let up. He caught both of Giles' forearms and gripped them. Kiev's arm muscles bulged from the force he was applying to Giles, who was now wincing.

"Let go," Kiev said, his voice steady. "The lady doesn't want to be touched."

Giles looked indignant. I thought he was about to fight back. He stood staring at Kiev for several moments. But then he took a step back and, scowling, resumed his seat by the fire.

I looked up at Kiev, unable to hide my surprise.

"Why?" I whispered.

Wordlessly, he walked over to a plate in front of the fire, bent down and returned with another skewer of sea vegetables. I looked at the one I had been eating, now squashed on the ground, and took it from him, still eyeing him suspiciously as I bit in.

"Why what?" He crossed his arms over his chest, looking down at me.

"Why did you just do that?"

"That should be obvious."

"Well, it's not," I said, widening my eyes at him.

"Witch, you were utterly clueless. If I hadn't interfered, you'd be in that vampire's bedroom right now. I'll accompany you back home too."

I didn't know what had possessed me, but for a moment I had been expecting him to tell me that he had done it to apologize for his behavior the other night.

"You pompous ass," I muttered.

I threw my unfinished skewer into the fire and stalked off.

Chapter 23: Kiev

Damn it.

Ungrateful witch.

My first attempt had backfired. It was disappointing, but my failure only served to fuel the fire to conquer the challenge that was Mona.

And the sooner I win at this, the sooner this nonsense is over.

The next evening, as soon as the sun set, I rushed through the forest to the bank of the lake and, discarding my shirt, jumped in. The clear water was cool and pleasant to swim in, and it wasn't long before I had reached her cabin.

I gripped hold of the edge of the wooden platform that led to her front door and hoisted myself up. Dripping wet, I knocked three times. When she didn't open the door after more than five seconds, I knocked again, more impatiently this time.

"Who is it?" the witch's voice called.

"Kiev."

"Go away."

"I have something for you."

"I don't want it."

I crept around to the large glass doors that opened onto the verandah. No sooner had I reached them than she ran around the cabin drawing all the curtains.

"Go away," she called again.

I walked back round to the entrance and entertained the idea of just breaking down the door. But I paused as my hand wrapped around the doorknob.

Wait. I can't do that. It will make her more hostile.

I continued to prowl around the cabin, looking through the windows for any gaps she might have left in the curtains. But she had done a thorough job at blocking me out.

In a last-ditch attempt, I degraded myself to begging.

"Please?"

Silence.

Angered that even this had been in vain, I brought my fist down hard against a small wooden table in the corner. Too hard. A crack filled the air. To my horror, the table gave way and fell to pieces.

No. No. Now she's going to hate me more.

I scrambled around on the deck looking for... God knew what. I didn't know what the hell I expected to find on that narrow porch. Glue?

The front door opened and Mona stormed out, wearing a short black nightdress.

"What the hell, vampire?"

Her eyes blazed when she saw what I had done. She ran at me, and although she wasn't heavy, the unexpected force knocked me back into the water.

"Go. Away."

The foundations of her cabin shuddered as she slammed the door shut.

Disheartened but still in no way defeated, I swam back to the mainland.

The first thing I did was seek out the ogre, Brett, whom she had appeared to be friends with. I passed a werewolf in the woods who informed me of the location of his home.

It turned out that Brett lived in a cave at the base of the same mountain I'd met Matteo at the other night. Mossy rocks surrounded the cave's damp entrance.

"Brett?" I called, my voice echoing off the walls.

A loud snore emanated from the back of the cave. I took the liberty of climbing through the entrance and saw the ogre lying in a heap on top of a bed of straw.

"Brett," I repeated.

He continued to snore louder than ever.

I nudged his back with my foot. When he still didn't budge, I grabbed his shoulders and rolled him over.

"Wh-what?" he spluttered, rubbing sticky eyes.

"I... I'm sorry to wake you," I said. "But I have a question."

He sat up, frowning, his yellow eyes still bleary. "Who are you?"

"Kiev. "

When he still looked at me with a blank expression, I said impatiently, "I met you the other night, remember? You came to my room."

"Ah, yeah. Remember now," he mumbled, leaning his wide back against the damp wall of the cave. "What do you want?"

"You're Mona's friend, right?"

"Mona? Erm... I wouldn't go so far as to say she's my friend." He paused for a deep yawn. "I'd like to consider her that, for sure. But she probably thinks of me more as her well-wisher than friend—"

"All right," I said, cutting through his rambling. "I'm sure you can still answer my question. When does Mona visit the mainland?"

"Once a day, usually. To visit the well."

"What time?"

"Erm… in the evening."

"And where is this well?"

"It's near the foot of the hill I took you to. Walk around that area and you'll find it soon enough."

"Okay." I left his side and retreated out of the cave. But before heading off, I remembered to turn back and say, "Thank you."

"Don't mention it," he grunted and slumped back down on the straw.

***

Early the next evening, I made sure to be near the well. I crouched down in the shadows of the trees surrounding it and waited. Brett had been right. Soon after sunset, I spotted the witch approaching, a wooden bucket in one arm.

As soon as she reached the well and lowered her vessel, I crept out from my hiding place. A twig snapped beneath my feet as I neared her. She whirled around and let out a small scream when she caught sight of me through the darkness.

"You!"

"Yes." I approached the well and leaned against it, trying to act casually.

"What are you doing here?"

"It's a pleasant night."

"What is this stupid game you're playing?" She paused, her blue eyes darkening. "Did Saira put you up to this?"

My throat went dry. Every part of me wanted to say yes.

But I couldn't.

"No."

"Then why are you stalking me? Is your life really so pathetic?"

"No," I said, my voice rising. "If you'd have just spoken to me the other night I wouldn't have had to do this." I paused, breathing in deeply to reel myself in and prepare my ego for what I knew I had to say next. "I just wanted to say… I'm sorry."

"Oh?" She cocked her head to one side. "For what?"

She wasn't trying to make this easy for me.

"For my behavior," I muttered. "Both on the ship, and also back in the prison at Aviary… And also for breaking your table."

I watched her face for a reaction. For any sign of forgiveness. For any sign of that frown softening. She kept a poker face as she met my eyes.

"That's it?" she asked.

"Yes, and I… uh… want to make it up to you. We got off to the wrong start—"

"Well, your apology is enough," she said, cutting through me. "I don't require anything more from you."

She heaved her bucket out of the well and turned to walk away. I followed her and grabbed the vessel from her arms before she could refuse.

"I'll carry this for you. Just to your boat."

She grabbed it back, at least a quarter of the water in the small bucket splashing out onto the grass.

"No, I don't need your help," she said, her cheeks flushing red.

"Look, you just dropped a load. Let me refill it—" I reached to grab the bucket again.

"No!" She swerved away, glaring daggers at me. "What *is* it with you? I told you, your apology is enough. You can leave me alone now."

But is it enough?

What will your answer be the next time Saira asks the question?

Chapter 24: Mona

Her heart beat faster as he touched her cheek. But she avoided his eyes. Their intensity scared her. She didn't know if she was strong enough to hold his gaze. Strong arms wrapped around her, and then a gentle finger beneath her chin pushed her head upward. She now had no choice but to face her fears. Her body responded to his embrace, even while her mind repelled it.

She'd fantasized about this moment for longer than she could remember, so she wondered why she was feeling apprehensive. Every movement of his body against hers sent chills running through her. She was attempting to focus her attention on anything other than what she supposedly desired most deeply.

I frowned at the parchment in front of me. I hadn't been able to sleep, so instead had decided to retrieve my story from the cupboard and sit down at my desk. The yellowing of the parchment betrayed how long I'd been toiling over it. I'd lost count of how many years had passed since I'd started it.

The words just dried up whenever I reached scenes like this.

The scene was technically accurate, at least according to my observations.

But I wasn't feeling it.

I wasn't living it.

I wasn't living my characters' passion like I lived their pain.

A feeling of emptiness settled in my stomach as familiar doubts assailed my mind.

Perhaps I'll never be able to finish this story.

Perhaps I'll never be able to give my beloved characters, Irina and Adrian, the love they've craved and fought for in all the previous chapters.

I pushed my chair away from my desk and stepped out onto the balcony, taking deep breaths, fighting to calm my nerves. But the emptiness continued to tear through my stomach, reaching its thorny hand up into my throat.

I gripped the railing, closing my eyes.

Stop thinking.

Just be silent.

Just be... numb.

Numbness. That word again. That word that had terrified Kiev so much that he was willing to suffer rather than experience it.

Numbness was what I craved.

It was the rope I used to climb out of the black hole I'd otherwise be trapped in.

Numbness was my savior, not my fear.

Chapter 25: Kiev

I never had been the kind of man to do things half-heartedly. If I bothered with something, I would damn well figure out a way to win at it.

I had more work to do.

I might have been out of touch with my social skills, but I didn't need to be a genius to understand that Mona still didn't consider me a friend.

And I didn't want to get Saira to ask her the question until I was confident that Mona would respond positively. I didn't know if the erratic wolf would give me another chance if the witch gave the wrong answer. I had to tread carefully, because I had no idea if Matteo would stand up for me if the wolf ordered me off the island. I certainly couldn't expect him to, and I wasn't in a position to risk finding out.

Now that I had gotten my apology to Mona off of my chest, at least that felt like some progress. My next step seemed obvious to me.

The following evening, I paid another visit to Brett. To my relief, I didn't have to waste minutes waking him up this time. I arrived to see him sitting at the entrance of his cave munching on a hunk of meat.

"You again?" he said, looking up from his meal.

"I'd like to know who does the carpentry on this island."

Brett's round face split into a proud grin, his teeth stained with grease. "That'd be me."

"Ah, good. I expected as much." I said. "You see, I'm in need of a small table."

"Oh? How small?"

I indicated the approximate dimensions with my hands.

"What for?" he asked.

"For... Mona, actually," I said.

Brett's grin widened.

"Got feels for her, have you?" he chortled, winking at me while wiping fat off one of his tusks.

"No... No. I-I just broke her table accidentally. I owe her a new one."

"Well, if it's just a simple four-legged table," he said, chewing thoughtfully, "I could have that ready for you in a few hours. I'm still on break. Haven't got much else to do before my round starts again, other than finish eating this beauty." He waved his meat in the air.

"I appreciate it." I was about to hold out my hand to shake his, but had second thoughts when I saw how filthy it was. "I'll be back in a few hours."

"In case you're late returning, I'll just leave it for you in there," he said, gesturing toward his cave.

I left him in peace to finish his meal.

My next stop was the beach. Remembering the shell Giles had

tried to gift Mona, I reasoned that perhaps he'd done that because he knew she liked them. When I reached the wall, I located the nearest exit to me. A vampire on guard duty sat next to it.

He looked up at me questioningly as I approached.

"I should be back in less than an hour."

The vampire nodded and let me out.

"Just be careful," he called after me. "It's never a good idea to stay outside these walls for long."

It was a calm night. A breeze caught my hair as I made my way toward the dark waves lapping against the shore. There was not a single cloud in the sky to dull the shining moon. The air had a purity to it that I'd never experienced anywhere back in the human realm.

I walked barefoot along the beach, scouring the sand for shells. While I collected some, I found so many objects of far greater beauty.

What a fool Giles was for bringing Mona a shell, when if he'd just strayed a little further, he could have brought her pearls.

Before I knew it, my pockets were filled with precious stones of all colors, shapes and sizes. Other than what was obviously a giant pearl, most of them I couldn't even put a name to. I lost all track of time. I must have walked for miles, enticed further and further away from the wall by the treasures I kept finding. It seemed like the further I strayed, the more gorgeous the jewels became.

I was brought to my senses only when I looked up at the sky and noticed its color beginning to warm. I'd been out all night. I cast my eyes back toward the direction of the gate I had exited and gauged the amount of time it would take me to get back there if I ran at full speed. *Ten minutes, at most.*

I still had time to bathe in the sea before I returned. I took off my clothes and placed them on the sand, careful not to let any stones fall out of my pockets. I waded into the cool sea until the water was up to my waist before diving in. I swam faster and deeper, enjoying the full stretch of my limbs.

Something smooth brushed against my foot. A dolphin surfaced in the water next to me. It was Kai. I'd spent enough time with him during my journey with Mona to recognize his features.

The dolphin nuzzled his thick nose against my chest. I wasn't sure how to react. My first instinct was to push him away. But instead I brushed my hand along his back, the way I'd see Mona do. He stayed still in the water, relishing my touch. As soon as I stopped, he nuzzled me again.

If only the witch were so easily befriended.

Leaving the dolphin, I swam back to the beach and pulled on my clothes. As I was about to head off toward the wall, I heard an odd noise coming from behind me. The sound of someone choking. I turned round to see a young woman crawling out of the ocean about twenty feet away. Her clothes were tattered, her hair a matted mess. Cuts covered her body and face.

"H-help," she croaked. "Ogres… escape…I… need… water…"

Her words barely registered in my head. All my mind could focus on was the blood that had begun to drip from her wounds now that she was out of the water. I walked closer, breathing in her scent. *Human blood.* My stomach flipped. I could barely remember the last time I'd feasted on a human.

"P-please… help…"

Within a split second, I was by her side, gripping her neck with one hand.

"N-no. Please! I need—" she squealed.

I covered her mouth and lifted her closer to me. The scent of her blood now bringing my senses into overdrive, I didn't hesitate for another moment. I sank my fangs into her soft flesh and drank deep.

With each gulp, I felt the life draining from her. I didn't pull away until I'd sucked her dry.

Grabbing hold of the corpse's leg, I dragged it back into the ocean. Once I'd swum into deep enough waters, I let go and watched it sink to the seabed. I hoped that some kind of ocean predator would eat the remains of her body before it managed to wash up on the shore.

Before climbing out of the water, I made sure to wash away all traces of blood. Though I supposed that I didn't need to worry about it too much. She clearly hadn't been a resident of our island, so I wouldn't face banishment for killing her.

My whole body tingled with energy as I raced back to the wall. Even the pang of guilt I felt over claiming an innocent's life couldn't distract me from the pleasure I was experiencing. Finally, I felt fully nourished. Animal blood simply didn't compare.

It occurred to me that the only thing stopping me from drinking from the witch up until now had been the threat of banishment. Had it not been for that, I was sure that I would have already claimed at least a litre from her. Granted, a witch's blood wasn't nearly as appealing as human blood, but compared to animal blood it was appetizing.

I reached the gate and knocked twice.

"I thought something might have happened to you," the guard said as he let me back in. "We had reports of ships floating close to the island last night. You were lucky to have missed them."

I hadn't noticed even a single ship all night. But perhaps that was just because I'd been so absorbed in my treasure hunt. Still relishing the aftertaste of the girl's blood in my mouth, I cast my eyes back up at the sky. If I ran, I still had plenty of time to travel to Brett's cave and back without needing an umbrella. I whipped through the trees and arrived to see that Brett had already returned from his night duty. He lay sleeping on his bed of straw. But Brett was a man of his word. As he had promised, a new table stood at the entrance. It looked just the right size to me, and sturdier than the one I had broken.

A smile escaped my lips as I noticed a grease mark on one of the table's legs. I ripped some moss from a rock and wiped it off.

Later that day, as evening drew close again, I walked with an umbrella toward the well. Carrying the table under one arm, I placed it directly in front of the spot Mona normally stood in to lower her bucket. I plucked two broad leaves from a tree and I spread them out on the table, emptying my pockets of the stones on top of them. After folding the leaves over the gems to form a pouch, I retreated into the forest—a different part than I had stood in last time to avoid her spotting me.

The witch approached soon after the sun had set. On reaching my gifts, she put her bucket on the ground and gazed around the forest. I had to duck and close my eyes so she wouldn't notice me. She turned back to the gifts. I watched as she unfolded the leaves and stared down at the gems. She moved them onto the grass and examined the table, picking it up and running her hand along the wood. Then she picked her bucket up and filled it with water. Balancing it with one hand, she picked up the table with the other and made her way back toward the lake.

I felt indignant that she'd left the gems after I'd spent so many hours collecting them. I wondered whether she didn't take them simply because she had too much to carry. I retrieved the gems and returned to my room in the tunnels.

The next evening, I placed only the package of gems in front of the well. But she ignored them again, even though it was clear that she had noticed them. The only conclusion I could draw was that perhaps she simply didn't like the precious stones.

Rather than have them go to waste, I gave the package to the ogre. He squealed when he parted the leaves with his fat fingers.

"Oh, my. Thank you, Kiev!" he enthused, gratitude shining in his eyes. "Gonna try using these in my carpentry… see if I can make my carvings more pretty."

For the next week, each night I roamed the island, hunting for more gifts she might accept. And the following day, I placed them in front of the well before sunset.

Sometimes she took the gifts, other times she left them. At first I felt confused—and agitated—that there appeared to be no rhyme or reason for which she would take and which she would leave. Though I supposed that I should have been grateful she was accepting anything from me at all. It meant that I had established at least some kind of rapport with her.

Still, I tried to use whatever observations I was able to make to better understand her personality, and improve my presents. It was only after the seventh day that it hit me.

While accepting a clay pot, she would reject a pearl. While taking rope, she would leave behind a bracelet.

At least one thing had become clear to me: she chose practicality over beauty.

On the eighth night, I was sure that I'd managed to find something that would make her happy. A dagger I'd found washed up on the shore.

But on the ninth evening, she didn't show up.

Unsure of what to do with myself, I waited around the well until late into the night. But when it was clear that she wasn't coming, I ran through the forest and stopped at the edge of the lake. A lantern hung near her front door, but no lights glowed through the curtains of her cabin.

Questioning whether I was making the right choice, I jumped into the water and swam toward her house. Climbing onto the balcony, I smirked as I noticed her new table in the same spot her old one had been. I bent down and placed the dagger outside her front door.

I spent the next few hours cleaning the exterior of her house, using coarse leaves I'd found on plants growing in the water. I scrubbed the windows, the roof, the railing… anywhere that looked unkempt. I worked as silently as possible so that I wouldn't wake her and give her yet another fright with my eyes.

After I was satisfied that I'd done a noticeable job, I dipped my hand into the water and plucked a handful of bright blue water lilies. I left them outside her door, next to the blade, hoping she'd find them in the morning before they became too wilted.

But as I swam back toward the mainland, I wondered if that had been a mistake. She might not have wanted me to pick her lilies. She might have preferred them to be growing in the water rather than dead on her porch.

That might have made her hate me again.

Chapter 26: Mona

What the hell have they been putting in that vampire's blood?

I still couldn't shake the feeling that Saira was behind all of this. After all, if it hadn't been for her hot-headedness, he wouldn't have been on this island in the first place. But, of course, when I visited her tree house to question her, she'd denied having anything to do with Kiev's behavior.

"Maybe he just really likes you," she'd said innocently, while knitting a scarf on her lap. "Maybe he's had a change of heart."

I'd scoffed, wondering how she could take me to be so naive.

The truth was, the vampire's attention unnerved me. Deeply. I didn't understand where it had come from, or why he was doing it. His own explanation was an insult to my intelligence. I'd spent the last night sleeping on a hill top, in the open air, because I'd felt so stifled. I wanted to get away from the island. Wash myself of its presence. Of *his* presence. Even if only for a few hours.

I didn't tell Saira or Matteo that I was leaving. They'd only attempt to convince me not to venture out alone. I told the werewolf guarding the gate that I wouldn't be gone for long. I ran across the hot sand and splashed into the cool waves. Ducking underwater, I relished the feeling of weightlessness for a few moments before calling out to my dolphins. Both came racing toward me, their heads bobbing up to the surface. I strapped them into the harnesses of one of the small sail boats moored in our port, and, gripping the reins, urged them forward.

I didn't know where I would go. Any direction would do. I just needed to be alone. I didn't slow down until I could no longer see the shorelines of any islands. I slowed the dolphins to a stop and tied their reins securely around a post. The dark color of the water surrounding us betrayed how deep we were now. I shuddered a little, reminding myself of the type of creatures that lurked in these depths. But at that moment, the solitude was worth the worry.

I lay down in the center of the boat and gazed up at the clear blue sky, the sun beating down on me.

I never should have accepted anything from that vampire. It's only encouraged him further.

I knew the type of man he was. Entitled. Uncompromising. Aggressive. If given an inch, he'd string it into a mile. He couldn't receive even the slightest bit of lenience without pushing to take full advantage of it. I couldn't accept any more of his gifts. And I could no longer visit the well at the same time each evening.

If I avoided him long enough, he'd grow tired of whatever game he was playing. And move on to badgering somebody else.

I closed my eyes, shutting out the world and relishing the sun's warmth on my skin. The waves rocked the boat gently from side to side, as if it were a cradle.

The gifts I've received from him in the past few days outnumber the gifts I've received in my entire life. And most of them can't have been easy to find on the island. He must have spent hours, maybe even days… Why is he spending so much time thinking about me?

I dozed in and out of consciousness, losing count of how many hours passed by. Despite promising myself to cast aside all thoughts of the vampire, I couldn't get him out of my head.

Why am I still thinking about him? I left the island to get away from him.

A cool spray of water brought me to my senses. I scrambled up and looked over the edge of the boat. Kai and Evie had started splashing around wildly in the water. It was only when I looked up that I realized why.

Oh, no.

A large ship loomed toward us at an alarming speed. *The Skull Crusher* was inscribed in thick letters at its bow. I grabbed the reins and tugged at the dolphins to hurry forward in the opposite direction. As soon as they picked up speed, I turned back. A dozen trolls armed with bows and arrows stared down at me from the distance.

"Hurry!" I breathed. My dolphins' supernatural speed suddenly seemed insufficient.

"Oi!" a voice bellowed down at me.

I turned around again to face the ocean ahead, hoping they hadn't already recognized me.

"Hey!" another voice shouted.

"It's that witch!"

Something hot sped past my ear. I looked in horror to see a fiery arrow embedded in the side of the boat. I managed to yank it out before the wood could catch fire, and threw it overboard.

Arrows continued to fly. I had to scramble around the deck

attempting to dodge them. They stopped only once Kai and Evie had managed to gain enough ground that we were out of reach of their slower-moving vessel. Although their ship was powered by at least a dozen large sharks, we still had the advantage of being small and nimble.

I breathed a deep sigh of relief, looking back toward them once more.

"That's right, witch!" one jeered. "Run away!"

"Just know that you can't run forever!" another bellowed.

"Don't know why they even call you a witch!"

I winced as raucous laughter broke out.

We'd made enemies out of the ogres on board the *Skull Crusher* the moment we'd offered Brett protection in our group. Brett was the son of their captain. Gentle soul that Brett was, he never did fit in with their crowd. They'd tried to make him perform violence he wanted no part of, and when he'd refused, they'd attempted to torture him into submission. We'd found him washed ashore on our island, beaten to a bloody pulp. He'd escaped by jumping off the ship.

They'd found out that Brett had survived, and they'd tried to reclaim him ever since. But thanks to Matteo's able management of our defenses, we'd outsmarted them repeatedly. The humiliation that came with their defeats only made them twice as dangerous to encounter in open waters.

Once I was sure that I was a safe distance away from them, I didn't turn around again. Instead, I focused all my attention on guiding Kai and Evie home as fast as their fins could manage. As soon as we arrived on the beach, I jumped out, dropped the anchor, and loosened the dolphins. Then I ran back to the wall. It was almost sunset.

The werewolf let me in through the gate, eyeing me with irritation.

"I thought you said you'd only be a few hours? Saira will kill me if she finds out I let you out alone for so long."

"I'm sorry," I said.

I walked back through the woods toward the lake, hoping I wouldn't bump into Saira along the way. On rowing across the lake and reaching the front door of my cabin, I was met with a long object lying on the floor. Next to it were a handful of shriveled lilies. Unwrapping the object, I found myself looking down at a steel dagger.

I hurled it into the lake, along with the dead flowers, hoping that Kiev was watching.

Chapter 27: Kiev

I was beginning to run out of ideas.

I needed to throw everything I could at her. I couldn't leave a single stone unturned. But the fact that she'd stopped showing up at the well after all my efforts wasn't a good sign. I had hoped that my gifts would have warmed her to me, not turned her away. As I sat in my dark room, I ran through all the hours I'd spent with the witch since I'd first met her. She was always so guarded.

But then, as I traced my memory further back, I recalled an incident on the boat, after we'd just escaped from Aviary. An uncharacteristic eagerness had taken over her eyes as she'd asked me questions about my personal life. About Sofia. I had cut her short, refusing to indulge in what I considered to be a senseless and uncomfortable discussion.

Thinking back, I realized that was the only time I'd witnessed any true spark of enthusiasm in her face. And she had looked disappointed when I'd refused to comply.

A plan began to form in my mind. I had no idea if it would work, but I was a man with nothing to lose. I stepped out of my room and exited the tunnels. I looked around the trees until I found a broad leaf that was dry enough for my purposes. Then I walked to the wall and crumbled off some of its chalky brick. Smoothing the leaf against its surface as much as I could, I inscribed a message. I read it through. Then I crumpled up the leaf, breathing out in frustration. I picked another leaf and started again.

Better, I thought, once I'd finished.

Next, I ran to the lake, and, placing the folded leaf between my teeth, swam toward Mona's house. I was about ten feet away from it when I heard a splashing nearby. It came from the other side of the cabin. Careful not to make a sound, I swam around the house's foundations toward the noise.

There, bathing in the moonlight, was Mona.

Her long hair flowed down her back as she tipped water over herself. My breath hitched when I saw that her shoulders were bare. Grateful that she hadn't noticed me, I retreated silently to the other side of the house. I climbed onto the veranda and placed the folded leaf between the gap beneath her front door.

I slipped back into the water and returned to the mainland. Crouching in the trees, I waited, my eyes on the entrance of the cabin. After several minutes, she appeared climbing out of the water, wrapping a wide cloth around her. I watched her stoop down and pick up my note. I ducked further into the bushes when she turned and cast her eyes around the lake. Her arm made a hurling motion toward the water. Then she hurried into her cabin.

Curse that witch!

I planned to head back to my room and try to calm myself down. But Saira came bounding toward me just before I reached the entrance of the tunnels. My sour mood intensified.

"Well, good evening, Kiev," she said, eyeing my soggy clothes. "It looks like you've been busy."

"What do you want?" I snapped.

"I just wanted to see how things are going for you."

"I need more time," I muttered, not willing to mention my failures. "I'll come to you when I'm ready."

"Oh, these things can't be rushed. I understand that. I just wanted to make sure you've been keeping yourself busy with the task."

"Well, I have." I scowled and turned to leave, but she padded round me, blocking my way. Her shining eyes looked up into mine, suddenly intense.

"You'll thank me for this one day, son," she said softly.

Before I could spit back a retort, she turned and galloped away. I stood watching as her large form disappeared into the dark woods.

Crazy wolf.

Chapter 28: Mona

I frowned at the folded leaf wedged beneath my door. I had no doubt that this was another one of Kiev's gifts. I shuddered. It hadn't been there when I'd left the cabin less than an hour ago. That meant that Kiev had been in close proximity while I was bathing. I hoped that he hadn't seen me undressed.

I was about to drop the leaf straight into the water, but curiosity overcame me when I unfolded it and saw that it contained a handwritten note. In case he was still watching, I pretended to chuck it into the lake. Then I hurried inside and locked the door.

I sat cross-legged on my mattress and began to read the smudged message.

"Witch,

I understand you've been avoiding me.

My conclusion is that you still insist on holding a grudge.

When we were on the boat together, you asked me some questions. I admit that I found them inappropriate.

However, if you want to ask them again, I promise to answer.

I won't come to you. You can find me in my room.

Or, if you prefer to meet somewhere more public, we could meet by the well, at the usual time.

Or, if you don't respond within two days, I could come to you…

Sincerely,

Kiev."

I read the note through several times. My cheeks grew warm and my stomach churned at his mention of those questions. I had hoped he would forget I'd ever asked them.

Why is he still chasing me like this? Is this his way of wooing me? Could Saira have been right after all about him taking a fancy to me?

I knocked the thoughts out of my head as soon as they had entered.

Don't be so stupid, Mona.

I threw the leaf aside and leaned my back against the wall. Stretching my legs out in front of me, I looked up at the wooden ceiling. I wasn't sure what to think anymore. I closed my eyes, trying to calm my whirring mind and obtain some clarity as to what my next move should be.

I could just go to Matteo and complain. Tell him to forbid Kiev to bother me again. That would work. Kiev would have no choice but to listen to him, or he'd be booted out of the island.

My other option was to meet with Kiev, and have him answer my questions. Although I knew that this would only encourage him to continue badgering me in the long run, I couldn't hide the desire that had reignited within me. I could always complain to the captain *after* Kiev had answered them.

My thoughts drifted back to my unfinished story.

Adrian and Irina.

They might benefit if I met with Kiev. Perhaps his insights might be what I need to finish their story. After all, wasn't that the real reason I asked them of him to begin with? To help me complete their love?

But, despite my longing to hear his answers, my whole body tensed with fear. I wasn't sure I wanted to be that vulnerable in front of him again, now that I had no idea if I'd ever see the back of him. I'd bared myself enough to him already.

I sat all day on the mattress, with nothing but my old towel wrapped around me. Kiev wouldn't seek me out before two days were up. I had some time to think things over.

Early next morning, the perfect solution dawned on me. I took a spare piece of parchment from my drawer and sat down at my desk. Picking up my quill, I began to write. I paused every so often, crossing out words, and trying to find ways to better express myself. Four hours had passed, with several more sheets of parchment used up, before I was satisfied.

I dressed and, folding up the sheets, tucked them safely beneath my shirt. Jumping into my boat and traveling toward the forest, I knew exactly where I needed to stop by first. Kiev had either forgotten to include his room number, or deliberately excluded it. Either way, I guessed that the ogre would know. Unless Brett's guard duty had changed hours recently, he'd be standing by the wall close to the tunnels at this time.

I was pleased to see that my assumption had been correct. Brett sat on the ground near the gate, humming something out of tune to himself and fiddling with his thumbs. His face lit up when he saw me approach.

"Eh, Mona! How are you?"

He stood up and patted me affectionately on the shoulder. I winced. Brett always forgot that I didn't like being touched. But I

143

didn't have the heart to correct him as much as I did Saira.

"I'm fine, Brett. I wanted to know which room…" My voice dried up before I could finish my sentence. I hadn't envisioned that it would be this difficult.

"You looking for Kiev?" Brett blurted out, a wry grin forming on his face.

"Uh… y-yes. How… how did you know?"

"Well, you've been on his mind a lot recently. I guessed he might be on yours too." Brett winked. "He's been asking me all sorts of things about you. Even asked me to make a table."

Kiev had that made especially for me?

"He's in chamber twenty-five," Brett concluded, still grinning from ear to ear.

"Th-thank you," I said, and hurried away, reaching up to hold my burning cheeks.

The lanterns flickered as I crept into the entrance of the tunnels. I looked around, but the place was empty. Most vampires had no reason to be up at this sunny hour. As I walked along the corridors, the only sounds were the odd dripping leak in the dirt ceiling and muffled snores.

Breathing heavily, I stopped outside Kiev's door. My throat felt dry as I withdrew the parchment from my shirt and bent down. As I was inches from dropping the sheets, my hands began to tremble.

I stopped, my limbs frozen.

Why are you even doing this?

This is a stupid idea.

Just walk away.

Somehow, the braver part of me took over, numbing my doubts and warming me enough to shove the letter under the door. Then I raced away.

As I reached the exit and ran toward the forest, I looked back at the dark entrance of the tunnels. I shivered, despite the mild breeze.

I hope I won't live to regret this.

Chapter 29: Kiev

I awoke to see parchment beneath my door. Rubbing my eyes, I got up and picked up the sheets. It took me a second to realize that they were from the witch.

How?

I opened the door and looked around. But as expected, she was nowhere to be seen. I supposed she would have visited me some time during the daylight hours.

Still standing, I began to read.

"Vampire,

I was going to throw away your leaf as soon as I saw it, as I did with your dagger and (my) lilies.

However, on realizing that it contained a note from you, curiosity got the better of me. I've never before come across a brute who could write in coherent sentences. Though I'm still not sure that chucking it wouldn't have been a better decision.

In any case, happily, I was able to make sense of your writing.

I accept your offer of a meeting. But not in the way you have proposed. If we meet, we meet on my terms, which are as follows:

You will not attend the meeting as Kiev Novalic.

You will attend as a man named Adrian Angelis. Over the course of the following pages, you will come to know Adrian intimately. I have attempted to detail every facet of his personality. I think you will find these notes quite sufficient to become him convincingly.

If you're not able to act as Adrian faithfully, then I reserve the right to cut our meeting short and never speak to you again.

I will be waiting for Adrian by the well soon after sunset, in two days' time.

If you don't want to meet me on these terms, I will in no way begrudge it. Just pass a note along to Brett for me rather than visiting me again across the water.

Sincerely,

Mona."

Fuming, I flipped to the next page.

"Adrian Angelis: lover of Irina Petralia" was the title of the character description. I still had no idea whether this man was even real, or just Mona's concoction. His name and that of his "lover" sounded ridiculous enough to make me assume the latter.

What I read on the following pages made my eyes sore. Paragraph after paragraph of sickly sweet descriptions of a man I was now certain could not exist in real life—only in the witch's frenzied imagination—covered every inch of the parchment.

"His eyes are the color of the sky on the first day of Spring. His eyelashes are dark, thick and curved at just the right angle to accentuate the shape of his eyes. His lips are soft as cushions, not too thick and not too thin. Just perfectly kissable. His thighs are—"

What nonsense is this?

I stopped and rubbed my temples for a minute before continuing.

I decided to skip over the paragraph-long description of Mr. Angelis' thighs, hoping the next part would be less nauseating.

Unfortunately, I didn't find any semblance of relief.

"Adrian is a brave man in every sense of the word. He's the type of man who risks his life for the woman he loves. He's virtuous and seeks truth in all circumstances, always standing up for what he believes in. He's the kind of—"

I skipped to the next section.

"He was orphaned as a child. He has no brothers or sisters. He was raised by a kind family of witches. Although he had a rough start in life, he always speaks gently, and he never lets his past affect the way he treats other people. He doesn't blame his past for—"

I tossed the papers on the floor.

She can go to hell.

I'd already made many degrading concessions in trying to convince the witch to consider me a friend, but this had stooped to a whole new level. I had no idea what kind of childish game she wanted to play, but I would have no part in it.

Although I was aware that I might be throwing away my last chance to win the witch over, I simply wasn't willing to pay her price. Furious, I ripped up the sheets of parchment and tossed them in a corner. I left my room intending to leave a note with Brett informing her of my decision.

But just before reaching the ogre's cave, a thought struck me. I stopped.

Why do I need to give her this message?

I will just go tomorrow evening as myself.

If she objects, to hell with her.

I ripped up my note and threw it into the bushes, then returned to the tunnels. I was glad that she had set our meeting after two days.

It gave me some time to cool off after her letter.

As nightfall approached on the second day, I dressed and left my room. As I emerged from the forest and approached the well, Mona already stood there.

Only, this wasn't the Mona I knew.

She stood wearing a deep blue satin gown, her braided blonde hair cascading down her shoulders. Pearl earrings hung from her ears, complementing her heart-shaped face. Her face… it looked different. I didn't know what she had done to it—I could only assume she'd applied some kind of makeup—but her eyes looked more defined, her lips fuller. She positively shone as she stood waiting for me in the moonlight.

I stopped, staring at her, stunned. I had no idea where she could have even gotten hold of such a gown in these parts.

I cleared my throat.

"Good evening, Mona," I said, finding my legs again and walking toward her.

"Irina," she said, looking me in the eye.

"Irina?"

"My name," she replied.

She didn't mention she was going to play Adrian's lover.

"Shall we take a walk, Adrian?" she said, smiling up at me.

I nodded and was surprised when she slipped her arm through mine as we walked toward the wall. Though she withdrew it as soon as the vampire guard came into view, becoming Mona as she asked him to let us out. But as soon as the door closed behind us, resuming her role as Irina, she held my arm again.

"It's a beautiful night," she whispered, looking out at the ocean. "Thank you for asking me out."

We walked in silence along the beach, and as we did, I couldn't help but keep glancing at her when she wasn't looking my way.

I walked in front of her, stopping her short. I reached one hand under her knees and the other around her waist and swept her off her feet. Carrying her in my arms, I looked down at her face again for a reaction, now barely inches from my own.

She was blushing, but more importantly, she appeared comfortable with my action, indicating that while Mona would have likely slapped me, I hadn't overstepped Irina's boundaries. So I continued forward. Now that she was closer to me, the subtle scent of her sandalwood perfume was more noticeable. For that I was grateful, because it helped take my mind off her blood.

"This dress is a little awkward to walk in," she said.

With each step I took, I was keenly aware of the shape of her body against mine. Every curve seemed accentuated as I carried her close to my chest, her arms wrapped around my neck. I had expected her to start asking questions, but she remained quiet, apparently enjoying the view as I walked through the shallow waters.

"I want to show you something," she whispered.

She tugged on my shirt for me to lower her. I placed her on the sand. Lifting the hem of her dress with one hand, and catching hold of my hand with the other, she pulled me further into the water. She continued leading me forward until we were waist deep, her dress billowing around her. My eyes widened as she reached for her gown's buttons and slid out of it, but I breathed out when I saw that she wore a vest and shorts underneath. She swam to a nearby rock and laid her dress on top of it. Following her lead, I did the same with my shirt.

I followed her as she swam further into the waves. The winds were high this evening, the ocean more turbulent than usual. While I was strong enough to barely notice the difference, Mona struggled against a stubborn current. I swam up behind her and caught hold of her waist, turning her to face me and pulling her into my arms. She looked up at me questioningly.

"Climb onto my back," I said.

I'm going to show you *something.*

Her arms reached around my neck, and the front of her body pressed against my back as she climbed onto me. I slid my hands along her toned legs to make sure they were wrapped tightly enough around me before lurching forward.

I swam with all the speed my limbs could carry us. I wasn't as fast as her dolphins—I didn't have fins, after all—but I was fast enough to make Mona... Irina... lose her breath. I swam the entire circumference of the island, and by the end, Irina was laughing in my ear.

"I never knew a human could swim so fast, Adrian," she giggled, gasping for air.

I swam back to the rock where we had left our clothes. Her undergarments clung to the curves of her body as she emerged from the water, her figure a beautiful silhouette in the light of the moon. I pulled on my shirt and helped her button up her dress, and then I picked her up again and walked back toward the gate. She leant her head against my chest and closed her eyes, her soft breathing warm against my neck.

She turned back into Mona as we neared the wall, insisting that I put her down and stop touching her as she knocked at the gate. We entered through it and walked into the woods. Her hand slid around my midriff as she walked against me. She placed my own hand around her waist. We walked that way until we reached the lake.

"Thank you," she said, her midnight-blue eyes twinkling, "for a wonderful night." She climbed into her boat, and before rowing off, she looked at me and said, "I'd like to see you again, Adrian."

I stayed watching by the banks until she'd crossed the lake and entered her cabin. Then I wandered back to my own room, replaying the events of the evening in my head as I walked. I hadn't been expecting her to want a second meeting. I thought she would have wanted only one, just to ask me some questions. She had barely spoken, let alone asked me anything.

I don't need to become that insipid Adrian fellow to win Mona over.

Mona. She was so different as Irina. Gone were the frowns, the scowls, the bitter sarcasm. In their place was just... an excitement for living. A lightness to her being. A freedom to her spirit. It hit me suddenly that Irina reminded me of Sofia in that respect.

For the first time in a long time, that morning, it wasn't Sofia or Natalie on my mind as I drifted off to sleep.

It was Irina.

Chapter 30: Mona

The moment I entered my cabin, I ran to my desk. Pulling out the pile of parchment I kept in my drawer, I flipped to the chapter of Adrian and Irina's first date. It was easy to find, because I'd never been able to start it. It was blank.

I wrote for hours, numb to the pain in my wrists. I didn't even want to change out of my damp dress. Removing it would stir the mist of the night's experience. I was afraid that a part of that night might fade from my being if I took anything off.

Although the scene I was writing was nothing like the time I'd just spent with Adrian, the words flowed more freely than I'd ever experienced in my life. It was as if my hand took on a life of its own and there was nothing I could do to stop the quill from dancing around on the parchment. Because the technicalities of the scene didn't matter—my mind had never struggled with that. It was the emotions that my heart needed to immerse myself in my two characters.

By dawn, I was sitting in front of a finished chapter, the exhilaration of accomplishment rushing through my veins.

Kiev had been good. Very good.

In fact, as much as I hated to admit it, he'd surpassed all my expectations.

I'd actually been surprised that Kiev had shown up in the first place to play this childish game with me—especially after those descriptions I'd written for him. Although my Adrian was a good man, I hadn't been able to resist exaggerating his characteristics just for Kiev. Because I hadn't wanted to give Kiev an easy ride.

Admittedly, Kiev hadn't behaved according to the character notes I'd given him. But I decided that I could forgive him for it. In fact, I was actually glad that he hadn't been true to them, because the Adrian I had described was unrealistic, and frankly, less appealing than the version Kiev had decided to play.

Now that I'd finished the chapter, I took off my dress and earrings. I left the cabin and bathed in the lake, washing the salt from my body. I dried myself and pulled on some more comfortable clothes.

Then I resumed my seat at the desk and flipped through my story, leaving bookmarks in the other chapters that I hadn't been able to start or finish. I took notes on a separate piece of parchment of all the emotions I needed to experience in order to complete them. Although the list wasn't extensive. It was hard to list emotions that you didn't know existed.

I walked out onto the veranda and brainstormed when and where I should go on my next date with Adrian. I decided that I would meet him again the following evening. I needed some time to wash and dry my dress so that it was ready. That was the one item I'd been able to bring with me when I left the realm of the witches, The

Sanctuary, and somehow I'd managed to hold onto it over the years.

I picked it up and smoothed it over the railing, frowning. The hems were already starting to look tattered from last night's escapade despite me trying to be careful. I'd need to try harder, because, other than my pearl earrings that Brett had gifted me, this was the only beautiful thing I'd allowed myself to own.

It needs mending as well as cleaning—another reason to delay my date with Adrian.

After I'd sewn up the gown's hem, I washed it and hung it outside to dry. Then I returned to my desk and wrote out a message for Adrian.

A much shorter one than I'd written to Kiev.

"Dear Adrian,
I enjoyed last night immensely, and I hope you dried off before you caught a cold.
    I would like to meet you again.
    Tomorrow.
    Same time. Same place.
Yours,
Irina."

Chapter 31: Mona

When I arrived for the second date with Adrian just after sunset, he was already waiting for me. He stood in fresh clothes, leaning his elbow against the edge of the well. On seeing me enter the clearing, he held out a hand. He pulled my hand toward him and placed a chaste kiss on it. Chills ran through me as the slight scruff of his face brushed against my skin.

"Good evening," I murmured, my heart beating faster.

He nodded, his gaze intense as he looked down at me. Without offering any explanation, he placed an arm around me and led me toward the forest. I had already made plans for this evening, but since he seemed to have something in mind, I decided not to interfere.

It soon became obvious that we were headed toward the gate. After seeing me struggle with a bramble catching the hem of my dress, he detached it and, gathering me in his arms, carried me the rest of the way.

Why do I insist on wearing this stupid dress?

We reached the gate unexpectedly fast, and I didn't even have a chance to ask him to put me down before the vampire guard had already seen us both. I blushed as the vampire stared at me in surprise.

He muttered the usual warning to "be careful" and let us out.

Once we were on the other side of the gate, Adrian started walking in the opposite direction to the previous night. We took a left turn and headed toward rock pools north of the island. He carried me until we were out of view from the beach.

"Wait here," he said, as he set me down on a boulder. He turned and walked toward the shallow waters. I watched as he prowled around, studying the pools, until he bent down and picked something up. He returned with a large white pearl. I reached out my hand, expecting him to drop it into my palm, but he ignored me. Instead, he walked behind me and, without asking for my permission, tucked it into the center of my braid.

Then he sat down opposite me and lifted his eyes to mine, a look of contentment crossing his face. Perhaps he was feeling triumphant that he'd forced a gift on me that I'd previously rejected.

His gaze was starting to feel more intense than I was comfortable with. But I reminded myself that I was Irina before him, not Mona, and I soon relaxed. I crawled across the rock and reached out to touch his hand.

"Does it hurt, being cold like this all the time?"

This was not a question I would have asked of Adrian, but I didn't mind because I felt hidden behind Irina.

He frowned at my question.

"You don't know if something hurts when it's all you're used to," he replied.

I stared into his eyes, my face now level with his as I knelt on the rocks, just inches from him.

He reached for a lock of my hair and wrapped it around his finger. He tugged on it, indicating that I sit down, now much closer to him than before. He reached for my neck and caressed my skin with his strong fingers, before brushing hair away from it, leaving it bare.

His eyes fell from my face to my neck. Tingles ran down my spine as he leaned forward and lowered his head to my neck, his cool breath barely an inch away.

"You're not wearing sandalwood tonight," he whispered, his voice husky.

My breath hitched as his lips brushed against my skin.

"Mmm," he groaned as he took in my scent.

His mouth pressed more firmly against the base of my neck. And when he broke contact, I realized what it was. A kiss. Then he leaned away from me, his eyes glazed as they met mine. I just sat there, staring at him, my heart beating at twice its normal pace.

I might have not known what to think at that moment, but I didn't need to know what to feel.

When he eventually escorted me back to the lake just as dawn was about to break, I wrote two chapters I'd struggled with for years in a single sitting.

He might not have been channeling Adrian exactly, but whatever Kiev was doing, it was working.

Chapter 32: Mona

Two evenings later, I once again found myself in Adrian's arms as he carried me along the beach.

"Over there." I pointed toward the port looming in the distance.

As we approached, we passed by the range of boats our crew had managed to collect over the years. I told him to stop once we'd arrived outside the main ship. I tugged on his shirt to lower me and we climbed the ladder up to the deck. Catching hold of his hand, I led him to the front of the ship, where I bent down and rummaged around in a large wooden compartment. I soon found what I was looking for: a heap of waterproof glasses. They were Brett's creation. He'd made a whole heap of them.

Standing up, I handed a pair to Adrian.

"Why?" he asked, looking at the object.

I didn't answer until I'd bent down to the cupboard again and withdrawn two knives. Recalling his cluelessness about how to catch food for himself at sea, I'd decided to share some of my knowledge with him.

"I want to show you something," I replied.

Placing the knives on the floor, I took his glasses back from him and said, "Bend down."

Instead, he wrapped his arms around me and lifted me up so that I was level with his face. I giggled and strapped the glasses tightly over his head, careful to tuck his hair out of the way so that sea water wouldn't leak into his eyes. Then he put me down and I pulled on my own pair.

Walking to the edge of the ship, I dove into the sea. Adrian landed next to me a few seconds later. I ducked my head underwater and surveyed the area beneath us. I was glad to see plenty of sea life surrounding us—different species of fish, crabs, oysters, and a variety of sea vegetables that Brett was becoming so expert at roasting.

Taking a deep breath, I kicked down to the sea bed and picked up a particularly large oyster. I surfaced, expecting to find Adrian waiting for me. But he had disappeared. I looked beneath the waves to see him hovering near a large patch of colorful ocean flora.

When he showed no signs of surfacing, I swam down to see what he was doing. Discarding my knife on the sand next to his, I watched as he ripped up handfuls of sea flowers. I patted him on the shoulder. He reached out and grabbed hold of my arm, pulling me closer to him. Wrapping his legs around mine to hold me in place, he brushed aside my hair and tucked a large flower behind my ear.

I had to surface for breath after that.

He appeared above the waves soon after me, with the flowers in his hand.

It seems that, once again, Adrian has his own agenda for our date.

He pulled off his glasses, and then eased my pair off with one hand. He swam toward a large rock nearby, indicating that I follow. I climbed onto it and sat with my legs dangling over its edge. I felt his chest against my back as he stretched his legs out on either side of me. And then he started work. His strong fingers didn't stop tugging at my hair until he'd finished braiding in all of the bright orange flowers.

He stood up and examined his handiwork. I couldn't help but smile at the serious expression on his face. *What is it with decorating my hair?*

Careful not to disturb my new hair style, I slid back into the water.

"You seem to like decorating my hair," I said.

He remained quiet, still staring at me.

"Why?" I persisted.

Ignoring my question, he slipped into the water. He positioned himself in front of me, his hands slid down to my abdomen and he gently pushed me backward until my back was against the rock. He lifted his hands up the rough surface either side of me, his gaze smoldering. My heart raced as his eyes fell to my mouth. My lips tingled. He leaned toward me, but it was my cheek that his lips caressed. I closed my eyes, feeling his kiss. Soft. Tender. Lingering. And just before he drew away, his teeth grazed me slightly.

Adrian knows how to avoid answering questions.

Chapter 33: Kiev

The door to my room was open when I returned.

Lorena.

The beautiful vampire leaned against the wall, her long bare legs stretched out on my bed. Her arms crossed against her chest, she was biting her nails with a bored expression on her face. On catching sight of me, she shot up.

"I've been waiting for you," she purred. "What took you so long?"

A sultry smile on her face, she wore a thin robe that drooped around her shoulders, the outline of her underwear clearly visible. Her scent was intoxicating.

I frowned at her.

"When did I give you permission to enter my room?"

"I'm sorry," she said, fluttering her eyelashes.

I opened the door wider and nodded toward it. She ignored my gesture and walked up to me, brushing the curves of her body against me.

"Let me make it up to you," she whispered in my ear, sliding a hand beneath my shirt.

I knocked her arm away.

"I'm sure there are plenty of other vampires in this place who would appreciate your company," I said, pointing once again toward the door.

Her eyes darkened. She reached her hands up and gripped my hair, hoisting herself onto me and wrapping her long smooth legs around me. She lowered her mouth to my neck and caressed my skin with her lips.

"Mmm… But I want *you*, Kiev," she moaned softly. "Don't you want me?"

Her teeth scraped against me as she shivered with desire. My breath hitched as she started tugging at my pants. I stepped backward, my back now up against the wall.

"No," I breathed. "No… Get out."

Her lips sucked on my skin harder, her fangs close to drawing blood.

I gripped her legs and broke their lock around my waist. When she struggled to hold on to me with her arms, I lurched forward and slammed her against the wall. Seizing her neck between my hands, my first instinct was to snap it in two. I managed to reel myself in and instead ran a claw along her throat, etching a cut just deep enough to sting.

That seemed to make her realize that I wasn't to be swayed.

"What is it about that scrawny witch?" she choked, her eyes igniting with jealousy. "You seem to have all the time in the world for *her*!"

She exited the room and banged the door shut behind her.

I backed up against the wall and slid down it. Sitting on the floor,

I stared at the bare wall in front of me.

What is it about Mona?

I wasn't sure I knew.

Chapter 34: Mona

It dawned on me that I still hadn't asked Kiev any of the questions I had planned on asking him. Somehow, those questions seemed irrelevant now that the words were flowing so freely just from spending time in Adrian's presence.

Since I'd requested another day before our next date, I had that evening free. After I'd washed my dress and hung it out to dry, and done a few other chores around my cabin, I took out the chapters I'd managed to finish over the last few days and read them again. I lay down on the mattress and found myself reading through the same pages again and again, lost in the scenes I'd created.

My trance was broken by the sound of the front door creaking open. I leaped up and my heart jumped into my throat when I saw Adrian standing in front of me. I cursed myself for forgetting to lock the door after hanging out the laundry.

His torso was bare as he stood in the doorway, water dripping from his dark hair onto the floorboards.

"Come with me," he said, his voice low.

"What?"

"You heard."

"No. I'm not dressed properly," I said, tightening my nightdress around me.

"I don't care."

I gasped when he grabbed my hand and pulled me out of the door.

"Hold your breath."

"Wait. No. Adrian!"

He jumped into the cool water, pulling me in after him. I surfaced, gasping for breath.

"I told you tomorrow!" I panted.

"I know," he said.

"So why are you here?"

"I didn't feel like waiting."

As he looked at me, I realized that something was different about his eyes. I was used to them being a dark blood-red. At that moment, they seemed brighter somehow. More alive. Or perhaps it was just the reflection of the moon playing tricks on my vision.

I splashed water in his face.

"You can't just barge into my home because you feel like it."

He grabbed my arms and drew me closer toward him until I was almost touching his muscled chest.

"Should I leave then?" he asked, his eyes fixed on mine.

His words were more of a challenge than a question. Unwilling to answer, I splashed more water at him. He swam backward and disappeared beneath the water. When he resurfaced, he was holding a dagger. The gift he'd tried to give me. He reached for my waist and pulled my back against his chest. Running a hand along my right arm, he intertwined his fingers with mine and stretched out my palm. He placed the dagger in it, closing my fingers around the hilt.

"Why did you reject my gift?" he whispered into my ear, his breath cold against my neck.

I shivered as his lips brushed against my earlobe.

"Why do you make this so difficult for me?" he breathed.

His left arm tightened around my waist, his right hand still enveloping my own.

"Watch it, Adrian," I said, trying to keep my voice steady. "You know I'm good with daggers."

Lifting my knees, I pressed my feet down against his thighs and broke free from him. I swam back to the cabin and climbed onto the porch. Walking to the bathroom, I placed the dagger on the windowsill before changing into dry clothes.

When I came out, Adrian was standing in the main room. I threw him a spare towel, forcing my eyes away from his torso as he dried himself. On looking up again, I swallowed a gasp. He had taken off his pants and wrapped the towel low around his waist. He walked outside and hung his wet pants over the railing.

"I didn't give it for *that*," I muttered.

But Adrian's attention had been drawn to something else in my home. Before I could stop him, he swooped down to my mattress and grabbed hold of the parchment containing my recently finished chapters. Mortified, I lunged for him. But he was far too quick. He flew out the door and within seconds he sat perched on my roof.

No. No. No.

I stood helpless as he began reading. *Damn vampires and their night vision.* Protesting was useless. It would only fuel his curiosity. I had no choice but to stand there, my cheeks ablaze, watching him leaf through my chapters.

When he had finished, he looked down at me. I'd been expecting him to tease me the moment he'd finished the first paragraph. Instead, his expression was serious. It unnerved me that I found it impossible to guess what was going through his head.

I crossed my arms over my chest and scowled at him.

"You finished up there?"

He nodded and climbed down, handing the parchment back to me. He looked out at the lake, and I breathed a sigh of relief, thinking he was about to dive in and return to the forest. But he turned toward me again before leaving.

When he placed his hands behind my neck, his fingers reaching into my hair, and planted a kiss on my forehead, it didn't matter what I was wearing.

Even in Irina's gown, I would have felt bare before him.

Chapter 35: Kiev

The more time I spent with Mona, the more I realized that I didn't understand her. And that irritated me.

It seemed that I'd already drained Brett's limited knowledge of her.

I needed to talk to Saira.

The next day, I picked up one of the straw parasols stored in a bucket by the entrance of the tunnels and walked out into the sunny clearing. I approached a werewolf passing nearby and asked for directions to Saira's home. Soon I walked in the middle of the werewolves' woods, my gaze cast upward, looking for the black-wood tree house that Saira was supposed to live in.

It was built a little away from the main cluster of houses, with a direct view out onto the lake. I wondered if that had been a deliberate decision, in order to keep an eye on Mona. I also wondered how many of my visits to the witch's house she had spied on already.

Although there was a thick-stepped ladder etched into the side of Saira's tree, I leapt up and landed on the small porch outside her door. Like all the tree houses, Saira's looked small and shabby, clearly built with whatever materials they'd managed to scavenge together on the small island.

I knocked loudly.

I heard footsteps and Saira's short plump figure appeared at the door.

"Ah, Kiev." She grinned. "What a pleasure. Come in, dear. Come in."

She swung the door open. The tree house seemed even smaller now that I was inside it. The interior reminded me much of Mona's cabin, bare but for a mattress in the corner and some basic furniture.

She gestured to a chair and I took a seat.

"So," she said, looking down at me. "Are you ready for me to ask the question?"

"No, no," I said. "That's not why I'm here. I want to know more about Mona."

Saira took a seat cross-legged on the mattress at the opposite end of the room.

"What do you want to know about her?"

A dozen questions ran through my mind but the first one that surfaced was: "Why does she write stories?"

Saira's eyes widened.

"Stories? I never knew she did."

"She seems to be... overly involved with her characters."

"What do you mean?" Saira asked, bending forward.

Somehow, I didn't feel like revealing to Saira the extent of Mona's obsession. It felt like something that was intimate, just between the two of us. So instead, I changed the subject.

"Why did Mona leave The Sanctuary?"

Saira sighed. "She said that she found the place too restricting. She preferred the life of a wanderer."

"She wasn't kicked out because she had no magic?"

"That's one theory." Saira eyed me. "But she hasn't claimed that. At least not to me."

"Where did you first find her?"

"Actually," she said, sitting back against the wall and making herself comfortable, "Matteo, Mona and I all met each other at the same time. We were all trapped in the same prison on the boat of some particularly nasty pirates. Matteo and I managed to break free from our cages, and we helped Mona too. It's made sense to stay together since then. We were able to hijack a small boat and make it our own. Gradually we've built up the crew to what it is today."

Saira wasn't telling me anything that I didn't already know from Mona herself.

"Why does Mona keep to herself so much?"

"She always has," Saira said, a concerned look on her face. "I've come to believe it's just her personality. She feels… uncomfortable around people and prefers her own company most of the time. But I think she's just been waiting for the right person to come along and offer her a little friendship."

I rolled my eyes at her. I was about to get up and leave but another question crept into my mind.

"Are witches like vampires—immortal?"

In all my years of dealing with witches, I'd never asked about a witch's mortality. I knew that witches on Earth died after several hundred years; they died of old age, unlike vampires, who were immortal unless killed by specific means. But I wondered whether witches in this paranormal realm were immortal, being in their natural atmosphere.

"As far as I know, they are," Saira replied. "Though to be honest the only witch I've ever come across is Mona, and, well, she's not exactly your typical witch."

That she isn't.

Unwilling to spend more time with the wolf, seeing that she hadn't been able to answer my questions satisfactorily, I got up to leave.

"I suppose the next time you visit you'll have finished your task," she called out of the window as I jumped to the forest floor.

Her last words caused my throat to feel dry. Just recently I'd been longing to get this duty off of my shoulders. Now, the image of Irina standing in wait for me by the well flashed before my mind, and the thought of finishing my task unsettled me.

I wondered if I might have been doing my task too well.

What if I don't want to stop trying to be Mona's friend?

What would that mean for her?

Chapter 36: Mona

He'd left his pants on the railing. Deliberately, I guessed—so he'd have an excuse to visit me again uninvited. Not that the vampire ever needed an excuse for anything he did.

The next day, I decided to arrive early, and rather than wait by the well, surprise him by showing up in his room. Perhaps I'd find him asleep, and I could disturb him as he had disturbed me the night before. I emerged from the forest, his pants tucked beneath one arm, and walked into the entrance of the tunnels. The place seemed empty on first glance, as I had expected at this time of day. But as I walked further underground, footsteps sounded behind me. I whirled around to see Giles emerging from a corridor a few feet away from me.

He raised his eyebrows on seeing me. Then his eyes darkened. I thought he was about to approach me but—to my surprise—he appeared to think better of it. He scowled at me and stormed off in the opposite direction.

"Good riddance," I muttered beneath my breath.

I continued walking along the corridors until I was outside Kiev's—Adrian's—room. I placed my ear against the door. I couldn't hear anything.

He must be sleeping.

I knocked.

No answer.

I knocked again. When there was still no answer I gripped the handle. I was surprised to discover that it had been left unlocked. I pushed the door open.

The room was dark except for a dim lantern that burned in the corner of the small room. And it was empty. A shirt lay strewn on his straw mattress, but other than that, there was barely anything else contained in that room.

I stood in the center, looking around at the grim decor.

I felt disappointed that I hadn't been able to catch him off guard. But more than anything I was curious as to where he would have gone in these daylight hours.

I decided to wait for half an hour or so and if he still didn't show up, I'd leave to wait by the well at our appointed time. I walked over to the mattress and laid his pants down near his pillow. Then I sat down and crossed my legs, staring at the front door and listening to the occasional drip falling from the ceiling.

After what felt like at least half an hour, I got up and opened the door. About to close it behind me, I felt cool hands slide around my waist. Whirling around, I found myself face to face with Adrian, his eyes staring down into mine.

Opening the door with one hand, he pushed me into the room until my back hit the wall. He placed both of his hands either side of me, trapping me against it.

"Where did you go?" I asked, breathing heavily.

He didn't answer, but continued to gaze down at my face. I hated feeling like he was studying me. I lifted my hands instinctively to hide my face from his steely gaze, but no sooner had I lifted them than he caught them and pinned them against the wall. He pressed his body closer against mine.

"What are you doing?"

His lips parted slightly and I thought he was going to say something, but then he closed them again. Finally, resignation flickered in his eyes, and he let go of me, taking a step back.

The silence felt awkward as we stood there, looking at each other across the room.

"I brought your pants for you," I muttered, pointing to them on the mattress. When he still didn't speak, I continued, "Adrian, this evening, I want to take you somewhere I've been meaning to show you ever since our first date."

His eyes remained on me as I spoke.

"It's probably getting dark outside already. I suppose we can leave now."

Wordlessly, he caught my hand and pulled me out of his room, not bothering to close the door behind him. As on previous nights, he swept me up in his arms as soon as we entered the forest.

Once we were on the other side of the wall and walking along the beach, I pointed to a rock in the distance. He ran toward it, and I tugged at him to put me down. Unbuttoning my dress, I laid it on a rock and straightened my underwear. His eyes roamed the length of my body as I stood before him in the water. Then, tearing off his shirt, he walked into the water alongside me.

When he motioned to pull me onto his back, I pushed his hands away and said, "No. Not tonight."

I swam away from him and ducked underwater, emitting the call that Kai and Evie had been trained to obey. It didn't take long before they came swimming toward me.

"Why do we need them?" he muttered on seeing the dolphins surface. "I can take us wherever we need to go."

"They remember the location of this place better than me," I replied.

I guided Kai over to Adrian as I mounted Evie. Adrian looked over the dolphin for a few moments before following my lead and sliding onto his back. Evie led the way through the waves, heading deeper and deeper into the ocean. Kai sped up until he was swimming alongside us, the two dolphins racing each other in the waves.

I looked sideways at Adrian. My motion caught his attention and he looked back at me. There was something wrong with him this evening. Something was on his mind. He kept looking at me as though he wanted to say something, but reined himself in.

We arrived at a formation of rocks far away from the main island. I patted Evie on the head, encouraging her to go the rest of the way. She swam in front of Kai, circling the rocks until she'd spotted an opening to a cave. I held my breath as she ducked beneath the waves and we resurfaced moments later in a clear blue pool, surrounded by rocks. Kai and Adrian surfaced seconds after me. I got off Evie and clambered onto the rocks overlooking the pool. I stood up and Adrian climbed up after me. The rock afforded us a better view of this little enclosure, and as I looked around I realized that the place had grown even more beautiful than before. Multicolored shells clung to the rocks, small pools of pearls and precious stones glinting in the rays of moonlight that escaped from the gaps in the cave's ceiling.

When I turned to face Adrian, expecting to see his reaction to the gorgeous cave, I found his eyes fixed on me, ignoring our surroundings.

"What is it?" I snapped. "You've been acting strangely all evening—"

"Mona." His deep voice broke through me.

Hearing him say my name sent goosebumps running through me. I looked up at him, bewildered.

"What? We're supposed to be—"

"I know. But I don't want to talk to Irina. I want to talk to you."

"Th-that's not why I brought you here—"

"I know."

Terrified, I averted my eyes, looking anywhere I could other than into those crimson irises.

"Why do you write these stories?"

A cool hand reached for my face, tilting my chin up toward him. Unable to bear the intensity of his gaze, I closed my eyes.

"Tell me."

Panic surged through me. I regretted bringing him to such a secluded place. There was nowhere to run. Nowhere to hide. Nowhere to escape from the questions behind his eyes.

I sank to the ground, burying my head in my knees.

He placed a hand over mine as it lay resting on the rock. Something about his strength lured me into a comfort that my brain was screaming I could never have.

I looked up at him, wide-eyed and afraid.

He kept his gaze steady. When I still remained silent, he reached to caress my cheek.

This is Irina feeling for Adrian.

That's all.

Shutting my eyes tight, I breathed out deeply and, trying to keep my voice steady, said, "Because feeling is easy in stories."

I looked up at him to see his eyes fierce with curiosity.

Not Kiev's eyes. Adrian's eyes.

This is Adrian.

"What do you mean, Mona—"

"Irina!" I cried out. "Don't call me Mona while you're touching me like this!"

He pulled his hand away from me and shot to his feet.

"I don't understand you," he said, his voice traced with irritation as he turned his back on me, looking out at the pool.

"You don't need to understand me," I whispered, my voice hoarse. "Nobody does. All you need to know are my boundaries."

"And what are your boundaries?" he snapped.

I fell silent.

I didn't know anymore.

Since meeting Kiev, I'd pushed my boundaries back inch by inch, and now they were unrecognizable. I could no longer see where they began or where they ended.

I felt lost.

At that moment, I was grasping for any bit of solidity. Anything grounding. I began to feel dizzy. I stood up and grabbed Kiev's hand, burying my head against his chest. He tensed at my sudden motion, then relaxed as he wrapped his strong arms around me, easing me against his body.

I felt secure in his embrace.

I hoped that just by touching him, some of the strength in his body would flow into mine. Strength I desperately needed.

I didn't know where my boundaries started or ended anymore, but I did know that at that moment, Kiev was my rock. Keeping me anchored in the storm.

I lost track of time as we lay down next to each other on the rock. I shut my eyes, listening to the steady beating of his heart. I breathed in the scent of his skin, stained with salt water. He rested his chin on my head, groaning quietly as he took in my own scent. As he ran his fingers through my hair, massaging my scalp, I lost myself in the comfort I'd found against the contours of his body.

His deep voice rumbled through his chest as he finally broke the silence.

"Mona."

I shivered as he said my name.

"Look at me."

Trembling, I looked up.

The heat of his gaze left me struggling to breathe.

He reached his hands to my face, his thumbs brushing against my cheeks, and before I could stop him, his lips were on mine. Unlike how I'd imagined a first kiss might play out, I didn't need to think. I didn't need to wonder. But perhaps that was just because Kiev was a man who didn't leave room for doubt.

What he wanted, he took.

I let out a soft moan as his tongue pushed through my lips. His mouth pressing against mine, he claimed all of me, not allowing me to surface even to gasp for breath. His hands slid down to my lower back, pulling me flush against him.

My lips danced to the rhythm of his kiss, my body in beat to his drum.

When he finally released me, I lay breathless, my hands flat against his chest. I stood up and stumbled back, staring at him in a daze, reaching up a finger to touch my lower lip.

His eyes still blazing, he stared back.

I suddenly realized how long we'd been out. The sky was

beginning to lighten through the cracks in the rocky enclosure. Although neither of us spoke, we both understood that we couldn't remain there alone any longer.

I slid back into the cool water, as did he, and we both made our way out of the cave. I ducked my head beneath the waves and called to the dolphins.

Shaking, I climbed onto Evie's back and gripped on tight. I looked back to see Kiev do the same with Kai.

We didn't exchange a word as we hurried toward to the shore. Evie rushed forward, and I didn't look back again until the sounds of Kai swimming became oddly quiet.

I turned around to see that Kai had stopped, leaving Kiev floating in the water.

"What's going on?" I called back, my voice hoarse.

"Kai," Kiev said. "He… doesn't seem well."

Panic gripped me.

I urged Evie back toward them but as we approached, Kiev and Kai moved forward again, although much slower than before. I wanted to stop and check Kai, but the sun was dangerously close to the horizon and we had to get back. We still had some way to travel.

I kept Evie going at the same speed as Kai, traveling at half their usual speed.

I was relieved when I felt sand beneath my toes. We'd entered the shallow waters just before the main beach. As I was about to jump off Evie, Kiev swore. I whirled around to see they'd fallen behind again and this time it looked like Kiev had dismounted Kai.

I rushed over to them, and as I got nearer, my heart leapt into my throat. Kai was floating motionless in the water. His eyes had closed, his mouth hanging slightly open. I gripped the large animal's sides and rocked him.

He didn't respond.

"No. No. No!" I breathed frantically.

My entire body trembled as I continued to shake him, hoping that Kai would magically start moving again. *Magic. That's exactly what won't happen thanks to me. The ogres were right, I don't deserve to be called a witch.*

I broke down. Kiev grabbed my shoulders and pulled me into an embrace, trying to dry my eyes and calm me down. But I could no longer draw comfort from him. His actions only made me panic further. I pulled myself away from his arms.

"Just leave!" I screamed at him.

He stood there, frozen, his eyes wide.

"Leave me! LEAVE ME NOW!" I bellowed at him until my voice broke.

He stared at me for another few seconds before stumbling back and moving toward the wall, casting confused—perhaps even hurt— glances back at me as he left.

Now that I was alone, grief took me. I caught hold of Kai's fin, and, mounting myself once again on Evie, travelled into deeper waters, dragging him along behind us.

I only stopped Evie once we were a mile away from the shore. Then I kissed Kai's head, my body racked with sobs, and let go of him, watching his motionless body disappear into the darkness of the ocean's depths.

Kai was just a baby in dolphin years. There was no reason for him to leave me now.

I took Evie back to shallow waters and got off her.

Still sobbing uncontrollably, I kissed her head too.

"And this is where we part, my baby girl. You need to leave me now and never return. Don't ever wait for me or try to find me again."

Although I wasn't speaking her language, I felt that she somehow understood what I was trying to communicate because she nuzzled her head against my waist.

"No, Evie. You need to be a good girl and leave me now. L-leave me."

I ducked my head underwater and let out a noise that I knew Evie would understand without doubt to mean that she was now set free—a noise taught to me by a mermaid when I'd first learned to train dolphins all those years ago.

I pulled my head back above the waves and watched as my beautiful girl took one last look at me. Her eyes were endearing as she gazed up at me. I felt my battered heart split in two. I knew she loved me and didn't want to leave.

And it was precisely because I had let myself love her back that she had to. I hoped that I hadn't waited too long. I hoped that I hadn't left it too late. I hoped that she'd still be able to live a full and healthy life, unlike Kai.

Evie slowly turned away and sped off into the horizon.

I beat my fist against my thigh until I caused a bruise.

If I had only let Kai go sooner, he might have been able to accompany her.

I crawled out of the water, and barely able to support my own weight, stumbled forward along the beach. I staggered beneath the morning sun until I reached the rock pools I'd once sat near with Kiev, and found somewhere to sit out of view of the beach.

I didn't want to be found by anyone.

I just need to be numb.

"Numbness."

Kiev's voice echoed in my ears.

My vision blurred as the sea spray whipped against my face, mixing with my tears. I lost track of time as I sat staring out at the waves. Closing my eyes and attempting to shut down my mind, I forgot all about Saira's warnings to not stay out alone for long periods of time.

Merciful sleep must have stolen me away at some point, for I was woken by a harsh tugging against my wrists. Both of my hands were tied behind my back. I felt a gag being stuffed into my mouth.

A sharp pain spread through the top of my head, and I lost consciousness.

Chapter 37: Kiev

The werewolf at the gate looked at me suspiciously and asked, "Where's the witch?"

I turned and pointed to her figure floating in the distance above the waves.

"She wants to stay out longer."

I retreated to my room in the tunnels, and, locking myself inside, lay down on my bed. As I gazed up at my ceiling through the darkness, I couldn't shake the glare Mona had given me. She'd looked at me like it was my fault her dolphin had died. I didn't understand why she'd thrown herself into such a fit over an animal.

I'd had to fight the urge to pick her up and force her to come back to the island with me. I'd wanted to take her back to her cabin and, surrounded by the silence of the lake, refuse to leave until she told me what was wrong with her. Until she made me understand her. But instead, I'd given into her request and let her mourn alone.

Now that the heat of the moment had passed, I realized that I should have seen Mona's wish to distance herself from me as a wake up call. *You've gotten yourself far too carried away with Saira's task. You're forgetting what you are, Kiev. Mona is safer without you. Continuing on this course now that you've kissed her would be like boarding a train knowing it's moving along a broken track. The missing rail might not come for this mile, or even the next. But it will come.*

I lay alone in the darkness for hours. By the time night had fallen, I found myself craving fresh air and a stretch of my legs. I exited the tunnels and walked through the forest. I passed by the occasional werewolf climbing down from a tree house, but otherwise I was in my own company. Perhaps it was my subconscious, but after about an hour I arrived at a pathway close to the lake. I looked out toward the witch's cabin. It was dark. Even the lantern hanging outside her porch wasn't lit. I'd never seen the lantern left unlit at night.

Worry clouding my better judgement, I slid into the water and swam toward the house.

I'll go up and listen at the door just to check she's inside. Then I'll leave without a word.

I climbed onto the porch and walked along the balcony that ran around the circumference of the cabin. All her curtains had been left wide open. I could see no sign of the witch's presence.

"Mona?" I called.

No answer.

Impatience and anxiety taking over me, I kicked the door open. I gazed around the dark empty room. I ran to the bathroom. Also empty.

No. She can't have been on the beach all this time.

I sped to the wall.

"Has the witch returned yet?" I demanded of the werewolf still guarding the gate.

He shook his head.

I stepped outside and cast my eyes up and down the beach. And then I started running with all the speed my legs could muster.

"Mona! Mona!" I shouted against the wind until my voice grew hoarse.

Guilt tore through my chest. *This is my fault. If I hadn't left her, this never would have happened.* I ran around the entire circumference of the island. I searched every corner of the beach, but it was in vain.

Perhaps she returned to the cave she showed me last night. My nerves settled a little at the thought. But before I could start planning how to get back there, a horn sounded in the distance. I looked out at the waves to see a large ship with deep red sails looming toward the island. Torches hung from the sides of the wooden ship, giving it an eerie glow. Two were particularly bright at the front of the ship, shining light over the words carved into its mast. *The Skull Crusher.*

Jeers and shouting broke out across the waves. On the ship's deck was a crowd of ogres. Outside the wall's gate, a crowd of the island's inhabitants gathered on the beach. Matteo and Saira stood at the forefront.

And then I saw her. Mona. Still in her underwear, cuts and bruises covering her body, she had been hoisted up into the mastheads of the ship. Thick ropes were tied to her hands and feet. She hung motionless, her eyes closed, and I feared for a moment that they had killed her already. But then her feet and arms stirred and I breathed a sigh of relief.

She is still alive. For how long, we have no assurance.

"Release her!" Matteo bellowed across the waves.

I dove into the water. Since I'd approached from a direction the ogres didn't seem to have their focus on, I hoped that they hadn't seen me.

"Hand over Brett," one of the ogres called back. "And then you can have this useless witch."

"Even if we did, what assurance do we have that you'll hand over Mona?" Saira shouted, panic in her voice.

Howling laughter echoed down from the ship.

"Just hand over Brett. Then we'll see about this girl of yours."

I'd dealt with enough creatures as vile as these ogres in the past to know not to trust them. They could lose their temper and kill her before our eyes at any moment.

It was what I would have done.

I ducked beneath the water, swimming toward the ship. I surfaced now and then to check that the ogres were still being distracted by Matteo and his crowd. As I arrived barely twenty feet away from the ship's stern, I swore. A sharp pain set my nervous system on fire. I looked into the water, reaching down to my leg.

Blood. Mine.

A thick black fin protruded from the waves less than five feet away. I'd been so focussed on my destination, I hadn't been paying attention to the waters around me. Now, as I gazed around, ten other fins closed in on me.

Beneath the clear waves, I caught better sight of my attacker. A giant shark. Its white teeth were stained with blood as it launched to attack me again. I kicked away from it, narrowly dodging its jaws.

I realized then how savage these sharks were. As a vampire, my blood should have disgusted them. Yet here they were, circling in on me, more and more being called by the scent of my blood in the water with each second that passed.

All right. These sharks want a bite. I'll give them a bite.

Clenching my jaw against the pain, I extended my claws. As the shark nearest to me hurtled toward me once again, I used both hands to slash out its eyes. Jerking wildly in the water, it swam round and round in a frenzy. I grabbed hold of its fin and pulled myself onto its slimy back, digging my claws into its sides so as to not slip off. When it tried to retreat beneath the waves, into the depths of the ocean, I slid my fangs deep beneath the skin above its head and yanked upward, tearing through its flesh. I did this repeatedly until the shark stopped its downward descent and drifted upward. *That's it. Obey your new master.* I gasped for breath as I was lifted above the waves.

With this vantage point, it was easier for me to take aim at the other sharks poising to attack me. I slashed out their eyes, one by one, until the remaining sharks seemed to recognize the risk of approaching me and retreated.

I repositioned myself on the blind shark, and, jerking my claws in a forward motion through its flesh, urged it to move toward the ship. As soon as we approached close enough, I leapt off it and grabbed hold of the base of the carved wooden shark beneath the stern. I winced as my body made contact with the hard wood. The wide gash in my upper leg still hadn't come close to healing, and it burned from the salt. As I edged my way around the hull of the ship, I just hoped that no ogres had heard any of the splashing I'd caused during my battle with the sharks.

Once I was directly beneath the spot where Mona hung—her eyes still closed—I caught hold of a rope hanging over the deck's railing. I lifted myself slowly until I was level with the deck. I looked up, measuring the distance between me and the ropes Mona was hanging from. I outstretched my claws in anticipation. Then in one forceful motion—my uninjured leg taking on most of the strain—I leapt up and landed against the ropes Mona hung from.

The ogres beneath me shouted in alarm. Two motioned to climb up the ropes after me. I slashed through the ends of the ropes nearest to me immediately.

I turned back to face Mona. Her body was covered in cuts and handprints where the trolls had touched her. I removed the gag from her mouth. Her eyes still closed, she gasped for breath. I slit the ropes binding her hands and legs, and, snaking one arm around her waist, leaned her against my body. Even after I'd freed her, she felt limp, weak in my arms. I didn't feel safe letting go of the ropes to make the leap for escape because she wasn't holding onto me tight enough and might fall down into the crowd of ogres.

"Hold me tighter," I hissed.

She made an attempt to tighten her grip, but it still wasn't sufficient to hold her weight against mine. Certainly not for the leap I was about to make.

Several fiery arrows shot up at us, two passing a few inches away from my head.

"Please," I urged, my eyes blazing into hers. I shook her body, and, having no free hand to touch her face, I placed a hard kiss on her cold cheek, grazing my teeth against her skin, hoping it would bring her to her senses.

She remained limp, a doll in my arms.

Several more arrows shot past us. The heat of one grazed my shoulderblade, singeing my wet shirt.

"Mona!" I shouted in her ear.

Desperation coursing through me, I made one last attempt.

"Irina," I whispered, "This is Adrian. Adrian has come to bring you home… Darling, please. Hold on."

At the mention of Adrian's name, her eyelids flickered open, a spark igniting in her hazy blue eyes. Her arms tightened around my neck, finally giving me the confidence to let go. I slit the final rope with my claw and leapt forward toward the ocean, holding her waist against me so tight I thought I might crush her ribcage.

Several more arrows shot past us as we fell. The shouts disappeared as we hit the cool water. Beneath the waves, I felt Mona slipping away from me. The force of hitting the water had loosened my grip on her. I was alarmed that she had made no effort to cling on to me. But much more terrified that the sharks might come again. I doubted I'd be able to fight them away from both of us, certainly not while my leg was injured like this.

I kicked down into the water and wrapped one arm around her while using the other to bring us to the surface. As more fiery arrows hit the water, I was forced to submerge us both again. I hoped that Mona had had enough time to catch her breath.

I propelled us forward, my eyes fixed on the shoreline, though continuing to dodge underwater to avoid the arrows. As soon as we reached the beach, I slid my hands beneath Mona and lifted her out of the water. As I staggered forward, the crowd watched me in silence—Saira had a shocked expression on her face, her mouth agape. Without saying a word to any of them, I limped to the wall, and barging past the guard, I entered the forest.

I walked to the lake as fast as I could and placed her in the boat. Refusing to look at me, she drew up her knees and buried her head against them. I took the oars and rowed us to her house, where I laid her down on the bed.

I looked down at her face. She'd closed her eyes. The frown on her face and slight quivering of her lip made me think she was still in pain. I lowered my head and pressed my ear against her chest. Her heartbeat was slow, but steady.

Brushing her wet hair away, I held her face in my palms. "Where does it hurt?" I ran my hands along her limbs, examining her skin. Although there were cuts and bruises, and a redness around her wrists and ankles where the ropes had rubbed against her, there didn't appear to be anything too critical.

"Answer me."

I stood and looked around the cabin. Opening the door of a cupboard, I pulled out a large cotton cloth and a white nightdress. Kneeling back down next to her, I tugged at her cold wet undergarments.

"Take these off." I forced her to sit upright, and held a blanket up around her. Slowly, she removed the wet underwear and pulled the nightdress over her head. Then she lay back down on the mattress and curled up into a ball, covering her face with both hands.

"Irina... Say something."

I shook her shoulders.

When she still didn't respond, I decided not to press further. *She's in shock. She needs space. I'll tell Saira to visit her in the morning.* Tucking the blanket over her trembling form, I planted a kiss on her head.

I cast back one last stare at her as I exited the cabin and swam back through the lake to the mainland. As I emerged—still limping—from the forest and entered the clearing outside the tunnels, I caught sight of Saira standing amidst a group of vampires.

On seeing me approach, she bounded over.

"How is Mona?" she asked, concern filling her eyes.

"I don't know," I said. "Check on her tomorrow. She wouldn't talk to me. But she seems fairly unscathed."

The wolf sighed with relief. "Thank goodness." She eyed my bloody leg. "That still hasn't healed?"

"It will," I said, grimacing. "It's just taking longer than I'm used to because it's deep, and I haven't had human blood in my system for... a while." I frowned, looking around. "Why are you all back here already? What happened with the ogres?"

"After you retreated behind the wall with Mona, we followed you," Saira replied. "Those oafs yelled and made a fuss. But frankly, they're too cowardly to attempt another fight with us on our own ground, especially when we're all fully alert to their presence."

I nodded and turned to walk into the tunnels.

"Kiev," Saira called after me. "Thank you."

"You don't need to thank me," I muttered beneath my breath.

Chapter 38: Kiev

Intending to go to my room and lie down, in hopes of speeding up my leg's healing, I bumped into Matteo walking along a corridor. On seeing me, he came up and placed a hand on my shoulder.

"Thank you, Kiev, for saving Mona like that. It would have been a great blow to lose her. She's like my younger sister."

His words cut me deeper than any shark could have, memories of the night I'd murdered Natalie flashing before my eyes. He removed his hand from my shoulder and walked away.

I limped along the corridor until I was standing outside my room. My hand shaking, I opened the door. I sat down on the mattress, wincing as I stretched out my leg.

Barely a few minutes after I had sat down, a knock sounded at my door. I breathed out in frustration.

"Who's there?" I called.

When there was no answer, I pulled myself up and opened the door. Giles stood outside, his arms crossed over his chest.

"What do you want?" I snarled.

"I need to show you something." His voice was calm as he spoke, his grey eyes fixed on mine.

"What?"

"You need to come with me."

Scowling, I followed him down the corridor. He led me to the open area near the entrance of the tunnels. Groups of vampires stood around, talking about the events of the evening. I averted my eyes when I caught sight of Matteo standing in a corner.

Only once we were in standing in the center of the entrance room—in full view of all the vampires—did Giles withdraw a hand from his pocket and shove it in front of my face. I stared down at his palm.

A pendant, old and rusting.

A pendant I thought I had left behind in The Tavern.

A pendant I couldn't afford to be looking at.

"Why are you giving me this?" I hissed, glaring at the blond vampire.

"Why don't you just take a closer look?" His eyes darkened as he shoved the pendant into my hand.

I dashed it to the ground as if it were on fire. Lifting my uninjured leg, I stamped down on it. It didn't break. I stamped down again. And again. No matter how much I tried to crush it into dust, the pendant remained intact, its rough edges ancient, but never broken. The metal around its center, not yet coated with rust, shimmered up at me against the light of the lanterns, as if taunting me.

"You don't like my gift?" the vampire whispered.

He picked up the object and, stepping forward, held it just inches away from my face. I jerked back. But he took another step forward, keeping the pendant swinging before my eyes.

And then I realized that it was too late. The border between present and past had been crossed. Tortured screams echoed in my ears—screams of men, women, and children alike. Blood soaked my hands as I ripped through their throats. As I cackled at their pleas for mercy. As my whole body quivered from the thrill of the kill. As my body was once again not my own, but that of my father. His pleasure becoming mine.

The words he'd spoken to me for centuries on nights like this replayed in my head.

Become one with me, Kiev.

My desire is yours. My pleasure is yours.

Willing differently will only cause pain.

Never forget what you are: my own vessel.

Chapter 39: Mona

I woke to find Saira standing in my cabin, water dripping from her fur onto the floorboards.

"Something bad has happened," she panted. "I don't know if even I can argue with Matteo to let him out of this one…"

My head felt heavy as I sat up in bed.

"Who?" I croaked. "What happened?"

"Just come with me."

She gripped my blanket between her jaws and pulled it off me. We both hurried out of the cabin and into the boat. Despite feeling weak, I managed to row us toward the main land.

I had wanted nothing but solitude. But the urgency in Saira's eyes had sparked something in me that I couldn't ignore.

On our arrival in the clearing outside the tunnels, a crowd of vampires and werewolves formed a circle. When I pushed through to the center, I gasped. Kiev knelt in the center, his clothes ripped and bloody, hands tied behind his back.

Matteo entered the circle and stood in front of Kiev, an ashen expression on his face as he addressed the crowds.

"We all know the rules. And Kiev knows them too. I'm not going to prolong this."

Mutterings broke out in the crowd as Matteo approached Kiev. He placed a hand on Kiev's shoulder and pulled him upright. I immediately regretted pushing to the front of the crowd. Kiev's face was covered with dirt and blood. My stomach flipped when he raised his eyes to meet mine. Gone was any sign of the spark that I had convinced myself was starting to show through in them. Now, his eyes looked dead. Numb. With pain, hatred or remorse—I couldn't make out. My lips parted as I struggled to breathe.

"In an incident I witnessed myself," Matteo continued, "Kiev attacked many of our crew members. He was not acting in self-defense. Indeed, nobody in the room had shown any violence toward him. He lashed out at Giles, who now lies severely injured in his room, along with several other vampires who tried to hold him back." Matteo paused and rubbed a hand against his forehead. "We simply cannot manage this island unless we feel safe in each other's company. Kiev's actions violate this fundamental understanding. Though we do not punish as harshly as The Tavern, this infraction calls for banishment from the island."

Mutterings of approval sounded out around us.

"I can't deny that I am deeply disappointed. I have come to see Kiev as a friend. An ally. But what has just happened, I cannot overlook."

I didn't miss the way Kiev's whole body flinched at Matteo's admission.

"However," Matteo said, "I also can't deny what Kiev did just hours beforehand. I cannot deny that he singlehandedly saved Mona from the clutches of the ogres." Matteo began to pace up and down in front of Kiev. "I propose that I give Kiev the benefit of the doubt in this case. The violence he partook in simply doesn't seem to fit in with the character he has displayed since joining us."

"I agree!" Saira spoke up beside me, an unmistakable warmth to her voice. "We should give him a punishment that is less severe than banishment."

Some protests were muttered while a few others made noises of approval. Matteo kept his gaze steady as he surveyed the crowd. It was clear that he had made his decision and nothing anyone could say would change his mind.

I had witnessed enough.

Whatever might happen to Kiev now—whether he ended up staying on the island and accepting a lesser punishment, or was banished after all—wasn't relevant to me.

Because the vampire with red eyes would soon be only a memory.

Chapter 40: Kiev

I trembled as Matteo spoke, not with fear, but shame.

A part of me would have preferred him to just banish me. I didn't deserve Matteo's mercy. I didn't deserve his hospitality or generosity.

I deserved his wrath.

I wished he'd punish me severely. It would have relieved at least some of the guilt.

The crowds dispersed and I was left alone with Matteo and Saira. I could barely look them in the eye.

Saira looked at Matteo.

"Do you have something in mind?" she asked.

Matteo gazed at me, apparently deep in thought.

"Yes," he said after a few moments. "Yes, I do."

"What?" Saira asked, seemingly more interested in my wellbeing than I was.

"Kiev, excuse me while I take a moment to discuss my idea with Saira."

I watched as they disappeared into the forest. They had to walk a distance away from me due to my acute hearing. It felt like half an hour had passed before they emerged from the woods. Saira cast a worried glance my way, hesitating for a moment before walking away, leaving me alone with Matteo.

"You can come with me now, Kiev. I'll explain," he said.

I walked alongside him as we headed toward the direction of the wall.

"I should give you a little background first," he said, clearing his throat. "As you may have noticed, the living conditions on this island are far from ideal, especially for us vampires." He paused and cast a glance sideways at me. "You're originally from the human realm… correct?"

I nodded.

"Then you may have heard of a place called The Shade?"

I gulped, uncomfortable with the memories.

"Yes," I muttered.

"Good," Matteo said. "See, I've never visited the place myself, but many of us around here know of it as a legend… Anyway, to cut a long story short, we want to make our own island like The Shade. Perhaps not as extravagant. To start with, we would be more than satisfied just having a witch who's able to cast a protective spell over the island and a spell of night over at least a part of the island."

We reached the wall, where a vampire opened the gate for us as we stepped out onto the beach.

"The problem is," Matteo continued, "witches are scarce outside of The Sanctuary. The Aviary has a few, and I believe Cruor does too, but they are hardly willing to share." He grimaced. "The only witches we could possibly have a fighting chance of getting hold of belong to a group of pirates who sail the ship known as *The Black*

Bell."

The Black Bell.

I smiled bitterly, remembering the night I'd tried to force information out of Mona about the ship. I reached up to my cheek, recalling the sting of her slap. So much had happened since, I'd forgotten to even attempt to find out more about the ship.

"They're a fierce bunch," he said, "and to date we have failed to even come close to plundering their island. Of course, it's protected by their three witches."

"So you believe I can help you with this?" I asked.

"It's a dangerous mission. More dangerous than most of us on the island are comfortable with. I don't know if you will be successful. But I do know that helping us with this will be a fitting punishment for you. And, of course, regardless of whether or not you are successful, the fact that you agree to help us with this will help you win over those who were against my decision to allow you to stay on the island."

We reached a small boat bobbing on the waves and Matteo strapped in a dolphin, indicating that I climb in.

"Tonight?"

Matteo shook his head. "Oh, no, this mission will need much more planning than we could possibly do before morning. Tonight I just want to show you the location of their island."

I sat down on the bench and Matteo took a seat next to me, clutching the dolphins' reins and urging them forward. Silence fell between us as we gathered speed.

My mind drifted back to the scene in the clearing. All those faces surrounding me, some glaring down at me, others looking on me with pity. And then Mona's face had appeared through the crowds, barely a few feet away from me.

So close, yet so far.

I hadn't been sure what to make of her gaze. At first I thought I had seen disappointment. But then she had turned around to leave, and she had just seemed distant. Indifferent to what was to happen to me next. Numb. My actions had just wedged a distance between us. A distance I wasn't sure could ever be closed again.

To think I came so close to unravelling her, only to have her clam up again. Or perhaps I never did come that close… Then I reminded myself that none of this mattered any more. *I should be feeling relieved that she wants nothing more to do with me.*

Matteo's voice broke through my thoughts.

"We're approaching."

His statement took me by surprise. The island had completely vanished from sight, but still, it felt like we'd barely been traveling twenty minutes. I had been under the impression that the vampires' island would be at least a few hours away.

I didn't say anything. I just sat watching as Matteo slowed the dolphins to a stop. I could make out only open ocean, except for a cluster of rocks nearby. I turned to face Matteo.

"I don't understand," I said.

"Oh, you'll understand."

Barely had he spoken the words when a thud erupted behind me. The boat rocked violently and I almost lost my balance. When I turned, my heart leapt into my throat. A hawk had just landed on the boat's stern. He shuffled his giant black wings and his sharp eyes fell on me.

"So this is Kiev Novalic."

Matteo walked past me and shook the hawk's hand.

"Glad you came on time, Perseus. I know the two of you have a long journey ahead of you back to Aviary."

Chapter 41: Kiev

"But before you carry him off," Matteo continued, "I'd like to have a little… word with him. Just make yourself comfortable while you wait."

My mind was numb with shock as Matteo turned to face me. His brown eyes that normally appeared warm and friendly had darkened to an almost black color.

He pulled out a dagger and slashed it down into my injured leg. I lost my balance and fell to the floor. He approached closer until his feet were touching my sides and looked down at me, his face contorted with rage.

"All along, you really thought I didn't know?" His chest heaved. "You really thought I wouldn't have found out about my own sister's death? You sick son of a bitch!"

He brought his foot down against the dagger, wedging it deeper into my leg. Bone splintered.

What a fool I've been to think that Kiev Novalic would be able to survive anywhere unrecognized. To think that the son of the Elder would be able to start over. I let my wishful thinking get the better of me.

My head spun from the pain. But nothing about Matteo's physical presence intimidated me. Even with that agonizing dagger piercing my leg, it wouldn't have taken much to overpower him.

But the look in his eyes had been enough to defeat me even before combat could start.

Pain. Grief. Loss. All still fresh in his eyes. Emotions I could see so easily within him, because they mirrored my own whenever I thought about Natalie.

"You have no idea how long I've been waiting for this," he hissed. "If the wolf hadn't interfered, I would have succeeded in ending you back in The Tavern." He reached down and sliced his claws across my face, cutting deep into my cheek. "Yes, it was me who turned Jack the human onto you via Michelle. I heard of your presence in Aviary when you first arrived all those months ago. I'd been meaning to seek you out ever since. And what a surprise it was when Mona delivered you to me on a plate."

He sliced me again. And again. With each blow, his claws struck closer to my chest. I lay there, letting him cut me to a bloody pulp.

I should have feared for my life. I should have been petrified that I was about to be brought back to Aviary, where for all I knew I could be reunited with my father and dragged back into the fiery hell that was my former life.

But I felt numb to any fear. Instead, I found myself welcoming the pain. No matter how much torment Matteo inflicted on me, it could never match the pain of losing his sister. I couldn't bring myself to strike back. I deserved every blow that he gave me.

Just as I was sure he was about to tear my heart out, a soft voice came from the corner of the boat. Where exactly, I couldn't see, for blood streamed down my face.

I half expected it to be Saira coming to my rescue again.

But no, it was Mona's beautiful form that I beheld. I had no idea how she'd gotten here, but I was glad to be able to see her face one last time.

Chapter 42: Mona

Standing at the foot of the highest mountain on the island, I breathed in deeply, inhaling the scent of the trees. I wasn't yet ready to return to my cramped house. I craved the open space that only a mountain top could afford me. I located the narrow stairs carved into the rocks and began climbing.

I hoped that no one would be up there at this hour, but was dismayed to hear voices as I neared the top. I was about to climb back down when a familiar voice said something that made me freeze.

"Did you see Kiev's face when I showed him this thing?"

Despite my better judgement, I moved closer until I could clearly hear every word of their conversation. Giles sat with blood-stained slings around his arms, deep gashes still visible on the side of his face. He sat next to two other vampires whom I recognized as being two of Matteo's closest friends and confidants—Pieter and Dominic. The latter two held cups in their hands—a bottle of rum perched between them—and Giles had on his lap what appeared to be a necklace.

"Rather you than me, shoving that thing in his face," Dominic muttered.

"Yes, well…" Giles said. "Matteo didn't go to all the trouble of retrieving it from the The Tavern for nothing. And I wanted to be the one to do it. Even with both of my arms practically snapped in two, it was worth it. You should have seen Patrick. He lost the bottom half of his right leg. Kiev ripped it off with a single swipe of his hand."

Pieter and Dominic shuddered.

"Did either of you speak to Matteo before he left?" Pieter asked.

Both Giles and Dominic shook their heads.

"What was the need?" Giles asked. "I did my part in allowing him to use *The Black Bell* as an excuse to take Kiev away. And he knows his next step better than any of us."

My heart skipped a beat.

"I'm still annoyed that the three of you left me out of this," Pieter muttered.

"He wouldn't have told you at all if he didn't need an extra person alert in the tunnels when Kiev lost it. Matteo doesn't want this whole affair to be public knowledge. It's a sensitive matter. You should understand that."

The men paused for a drink.

"Wasn't I right about Saira?" Dominic said.

"Oh, shut up," Giles said, nudging his shoulder and wincing as soon as he made contact. "It was obvious to all of us as soon as she rescued Kiev that she was going to be an obstacle."

"I still don't understand why Matteo waited so long," Pieter said. "He should have just finished Kiev as soon as he set foot on the island."

"Well, it took a while to track down Perseus."

"He didn't need Perseus," Pieter said. "We could have helped Matteo kill him."

"Yes, but Matteo wanted to do this right the second time. He knows Kiev will suffer more if taken back to Aviary. A quick death from us would be too light a punishment in his eyes."

"He also knows that both Saira and Mona developed a liking for Kiev," Dominic said. "Matteo couldn't just swipe him away for no good reason without upsetting them... and you know how important they are to him. Especially Mona."

Giles looked out toward the ocean. I didn't miss the scowl on his face as soon as Dominic mentioned my name.

"Do you think he made a mistake?" Pieter asked.

"Mistake?"

Pieter paused for a few moments, hesitating before opening his mouth again. "Telling us to leave him alone with that bastard."

"Well, he's not going to be alone with him for long, is he?" Giles grinned from ear to ear.

Pieter nodded. "I suppose not."

"Once he does reach the eastern border of Triquetra, there's no reason to fear for him. Hawks don't like to wait around..."

They continued talking, but I could no longer make sense of the words entering my ears. The vibrating of four words took over my mind and senses.

They pounded through my brain, replaying over and over again.

Kiev.

Hawk.

Eastern border.

When Saira had approached me with news of Kiev's pending execution back at The Tavern, I had hesitated. Indeed, I had thought it better we left him behind.

But now, after hearing those three vampires gossiping on the mountain, there was no thinking to be done. My brain shut down. In its place was sheer adrenaline. I knew where the location was. What I didn't know was whether I would be able to get there on time. I rushed through the gate, ignoring the protests of the guard, and stumbled out across the sand.

Tears streamed down my cheeks as I ran. Tears of uncertainty. Tears of fear over the consequences of this reckless action.

But I couldn't stop myself from running.

I reached the port and found a dolphin swimming near the main ship. I had no time to find a boat and harness it in. I dove into the water and mounted it directly.

"Hurry," I whispered as the dolphin sped through the waves.

When I approached the narrow rock formation that marked Triquetra's eastern border, a small boat came into view. Both relief and terror rushed through me at once. On reaching it, I gripped the edge of the boat and hauled myself over.

I clasped a hand over my mouth to swallow a scream. Kiev lay on the deck in a pool of his own blood, barely breathing. Matteo stood looming over him, slashing his skin to the point where Kiev was becoming unrecognizable.

"Matteo!"

I rushed forward and flung myself at Matteo. He whirled around, sliding me off him, and stared down at me. The darkness in his eyes made me stumble back. I'd never seen Matteo in such a state before in all the years I had known him.

"Wh-what the hell are you doing?" I gasped, grabbing on to his arm.

Matteo's face contorted with irritation as he shook me away. He seemed to struggle for a moment whether to ignore my presence and go back to maiming Kiev. He lowered his blood-soaked claws. "Exactly what this man deserves." His deep voice trembled as he spoke.

"What? But you said—"

"This monster killed my sister! She was madly in love with him. And he murdered her while she was helpless!" Matteo slammed his hands down against the side of the boat, the force of his motion rocking the boat dangerously from side to side.

His words knocked me breathless.

I stared at Kiev's barely breathing form, unsure of what to think. What to believe. What to feel.

Just an hour ago, I would have wanted to believe that Kiev was a murderer. It would have made it easier to rebuild my walls to their former height, brick by brick. But now all I felt was fear.

As I looked down into his tortured eyes, the truth came crashing down on me. I had let him strip me away, layer by layer, and now that I found myself standing before him almost naked, I wondered what kind of a person I had allowed to behold me.

What if I've made a mistake even coming here?

What if he doesn't deserve to be saved?

As Matteo barged past, brushing me aside to launch himself at Kiev once again, my knees buckled. I collapsed in a corner, barely paying attention to the hawk sitting a few feet away from me. Conflicting emotions erupted within me all at once. So many things about the situation didn't make sense to me. But most of all, I didn't understand why Kiev wasn't fighting back. *Why is he just lying there?*

Matteo stopped his renewed tirade of blows and gripped Kiev's neck, pulling him into standing position. I watched as the two men looked into each other's eyes.

"I just need you to know"—the words escaped Kiev's lips in a rasping whisper—"that I loved your sister."

"Bastard! Shut your mouth! Shut your lying m—"

Matteo choked mid-sentence and, letting go of Kiev, fell to his knees. His hands balled into fists as he crashed them down against the floorboards. He continued beating the floor until his hands were a bloody mess. Tears streaming from his eyes, his entire body trembling and racked with sobs, he dropped his head to the floor and lost himself to grief.

Kiev fell beside him, clutching his leg, his eyes still fixed on Matteo. "I can't expect you to ever forgive me. Kill me now, or send me back to Aviary. But… I just need you to know that I loved your sister. I loved Natalie… until her last breath."

Then Kiev shed tears of his own. They dripped down his face slowly, then all at once, mixing with blood and dirt. Minutes passed by as the two men lay on the ground shaking, their hearts suffering as one.

"N-no, Kiev," Matteo managed finally, looking up at him, pain traced in his eyes.

Kiev stared at him in bewilderment.

"God knows I don't want to believe it," Matteo said. "I want to believe you're a cold-blooded killer. I want to believe that you meant to kill Natalie and that you enjoyed every damn second of it. But no matter how hard I've tried to convince myself… I-I can't see it in your eyes. I just can't see it in those cursed eyes."

"What?" Kiev breathed, his voice choked up. "I killed your sister, for Christ's sake."

"Don't think a second goes by when I forget it," Matteo said, wincing. "But of creatures who inhabit the darkness, there are two types. Those who revel in it, and those who fight to escape it."

Kiev continued to stare at Matteo, inhaling a sharp breath.

"The Elders have cast their shadow over many lives," Matteo said, his eyes darkening. "I should know. I was once a child of the same evil that inhabited you for centuries. I can't ever forget what it felt like to hold absolute belief that I was incapable of disobeying my father." Clenching his fists, he shivered. "It's a hold that makes a person believe he is no longer capable of goodness, and so he simply stops attempting to fight the darkness. Until—by some mercy—a glimmer of hope sparks from a fire outside of him. A hope that springs alive, and eventually has the power to transform if he cares to guard it enough…"

Matteo paused, his eyes glazing over as he drifted off somewhere else.

"No," he murmured after a few moments, his bloodshot eyes becoming focussed again. "I don't think that damning you is my path to solace."

Overwhelmed and worn down by the clashing emotions firing from all three of our hearts, it was my turn to break down into tears, sobbing alongside the two men. I forgot myself as I partook in their grief with abandon.

Without thinking, I walked over to Matteo, kissed his cheek, and cradled his head in my arms. Though tears still dripped from his eyes, he looked shocked by my display of affection. Indeed it was the first time I'd ever so much as touched him since I'd known him. Then, drawing out the dagger from my belt, I ripped a piece of fabric from the end of my nightdress. I dipped it into the fresh water barrel stored nearby, and wiped the blood away from Kiev's injured face. At least now that Matteo had stopped cutting him, his shallower wounds were beginning to heal.

The hawk sitting in the corner of the boat shuffled his wings. He eyed the two vampires with contempt.

"What's going on?" he asked, glaring at Matteo. "I'm tired of waiting."

He spread his wings and walked toward us, his eyes set on Kiev. I stood up and brandished my dagger, forcing him to take a step back.

"I... I've changed my mind, Perseus," Matteo said, gathering himself to his feet. "You're no longer needed."

The hawk let out a furious shriek and flew at Matteo. I didn't understand how he found the strength, but Kiev shot up and tore a gash through Perseus' wing with his claws before the bird could reach Matteo. The hawk screamed with pain, then set his eyes again on Kiev, attempting to grip him within his talons.

"We have to finish him!" Matteo panted. "If we let him escape, he'll return to Aviary and inform all the others of your whereabouts. Then none of us will be safe."

The hawk shook himself free from both vampires. Then he turned his angry eyes on me.

In one swift motion, I found myself being lifted into the air, sharp talons digging into my arms. I was too alarmed to even scream. The one thought that circled my mind as Perseus began his ascent was that if he planned to take me back to Aviary, perhaps it was for the best.

Chapter 43: Kiev

The sight of the hawk carrying away Mona set my body on fire. Adrenaline coursed through me as I yanked out Matteo's dagger from my leg. With all the strength my wrecked body could muster, I leapt upward. Perseus shrieked as my claws dug into him for grip.

Gripping the dagger, I sliced through the talon nearest me. The hawk's shrieks grew so loud it felt like my ear drums were about to explode. Weakened, he released his hold on Mona. She fell down and hit the water with a splash. I trusted she'd make it to the boat where Matteo would assist her.

Then I attempted to cut the remaining talon. As I reached across, the hawk's sharp beak shot down and cut through my hand, making me lose hold of the dagger. As I clung to the irate hawk with one hand, my claws felt dangerously close to losing their grip.

I can't let him get away.

I knew the consequences that his escape would bring about. I couldn't bring that kind of misfortune upon Matteo's island. *Death would be less painful than bearing that guilt.*

I dug my free hand into the swaying body of the hawk and achieved a better grip. Slowly and steadily, attempting to avoid the hawk's beak, which kept stabbing down, trying to main me, I worked my way round his body until I reached his back where I positioned myself between his two giant wings. He continued to writhe in the air. Though severely injured, Perseus was still a fiercely strong creature—especially now that he was angered. He was vengeful as a raging bull.

I lifted myself up directly behind his neck. Grabbing hold of one of his wings, I poised myself to slice right through it. But he lunged down, making me lose my grip. I slid off his back, and were it not for my lightning-fast reflexes grabbing hold of his remaining talon at the last minute, he would have escaped.

Again, I attempted to climb up, one hand after the other.

"Don't even think about it." His beak pierced down, this time catching my arm and digging into my flesh. Groaning, I once again found myself hanging from one arm. I was keenly aware of our rapid ascent. The hawk climbed higher by the second, his wings working furiously. We were now so high I could barely see the sea through the clouds any more.

If I didn't end this battle soon and I let him reach land, even if I killed him, I would lose my own life. There were only so many feet a vampire could fall without being fatally wounded.

And dawn was close. Too close. As soon as the sun rose, I would have lost the battle.

I have to kill him now, or die trying.

Chapter 44: Mona

Although no part of me doubted his prowess, my mind was alight with panic that Kiev still hadn't returned. To make matters worse, I could no longer see either of them in the sky, and all sounds of their struggle had vanished.

The sea chilled me to the bone. I knew these waters were dangerous just from the temperature. Deep waters in these parts were never safe. There were all sorts of sea predators. I ducked my head under the water and called for the dolphin, relieved when he came to me.

"Mona! Get back in the boat," Matteo called. "It's not safe, even with the dolphin. You can wait for Kiev here with me."

I ignored Matteo and continued to zigzag in the waves, my head tilted upward as I scanned the skies. The clouds broke every so often to reveal the full moon, but otherwise it was a black night.

"Kiev!" I found myself yelling up at the heavens.

Matteo approached me in the boat and extended a hand down to me. Although I was now shivering, I shook my head. Leaving the water felt like one step toward defeat. Leaving the water felt like letting go.

Matteo followed me in the boat as I moved forward. His strong arms grabbed me by my shoulders and he pulled me onto the boat. He sat me down on a bench in the corner and, retrieving a blanket from one of the cabinets, wrapped it around me, rubbing my shoulders as he did.

"We'll wait here until he returns," Matteo whispered, placing a kiss on the top of my head.

Normally I would have flinched at Matteo's affection but right now, I found myself grasping for any comfort I could hold onto. I looked into his eyes and saw that he was earnest in his promise.

"But what if he doesn't?" I asked, my voice shaking.

Matteo sat down next to me and breathed out deeply.

"I believe he will return."

We sat in silence. The events of the last few hours seemed to be a blur as my mind was still trying to process them.

"So it was you all along," I croaked. "It was you who caused Kiev trouble back at The Tavern. You who set Giles on Kiev in the tunnels. All of your friendliness was an act…"

Matteo nodded.

"I suppose I've never told you that I was an actor—part of a theater—before I was turned," he said, his eyes downcast. "It sure as hell wasn't easy, but I played my part well."

"And the hawk? How did you—?" I asked.

"Perseus…" Matteo muttered, rubbing his forehead. "An old acquaintance. He betrayed Aviary many years ago and became an outcast. But I knew he was desperate to return. Once I'd managed to track him down, it wasn't difficult to convince him that bringing

Kiev back there would be the best way to win back Aviary's trust."

I realized now how rarely I had seen Matteo around the island recently. I had been too wrapped up with Adrian to notice it before.

I stood up and looked out toward the ocean once again. The sky was still empty. I turned back to Matteo, my voice starting to feel more constricted as each second passed.

"Are you really still considering provoking the vampires of *The Black Bell*, or was that just a guise?"

"How could we not still dream about claiming one of their witches?" Matteo heaved a sigh. "I don't think we'll ever be able to forget about it. But I'm not going to force Kiev to take part in the mission if he doesn't want to."

Silence fell between us and tears threatened to drip from Matteo's eyes again. He brushed his hand against his face to catch them. I found my hand reaching for Matteo's shoulder and giving it a squeeze.

"Something has changed in you, Mona," Matteo said softly. I withdrew my hand from his shoulder in a flash. "Ever since that vampire entered your life, you've been behaving differently."

I stood up and walked to the opposite end of the boat, clutching the blanket closer around my shoulders. I shivered as I looked out at the empty waters, which were beginning to reflect a deep orange glow emanating from the skyline. I continued standing there, away from Matteo. Away from the pressure to voice what I knew I couldn't. I stood in the same spot until the tip of the orange sun peeked out from behind the horizon.

I don't know myself any more.

I should be hoping that Kiev won't return.

But with the dawn came Kiev.

Chapter 45: Mona

I gasped on seeing him drop from the sky—followed by the dead body of the hawk—and swim toward us. Matteo reached out and hauled him onto the boat. I could see that he was bleeding badly, but I avoided looking at his face. Now that the sun's rays were breaking through the clouds, the two vampires sat beneath the covering at the center of the boat. They exchanged words in low voices as we headed back toward the island.

I remained standing at the front of the boat. I closed my eyes, hoping the wind would calm the flames burning me up inside.

When we arrived back on the island's beach, a strong hand gripped my arm and pulled me beneath the covering. I didn't need to look up to know that it was Kiev. Eyeing us, Matteo sighed and picked a large parasol. Careful to shield himself from the sun, he left the boat. I looked after Matteo with desperate eyes.

No, captain. Don't go. Not now.

I trembled as Kiev held me.

"I'm sorry," he muttered.

I felt my lips quiver as I continued to avert my eyes.

"For what?" I choked.

"For not telling you about my past... about Natalie."

"You had no reason to tell me," I said, trying to summon every bit of willpower I had left in me to not let him hear my voice break.

He breathed out a frustrated sigh.

"Look, I'm tired of playing games. And I'm damn tired of letting the past keep chains on me. I know you want nothing more to do with me now. And I'm glad. But I ask you to tell me one thing...just to put my curiosity to rest. Was it Mona or Irina I kissed?"

His words gutted me like a blade in a fish.

"Wh-what are you talking about?" I yanked my arm away from his grasp and turned my back on him. Closing my eyes tight in an attempt to lock in the tears, I swallowed, my throat dangerously dry, and said, "I'm sorry you ever had any confusion about that."

I paused, breathing out deeply before attempting to speak again.

He walked up to me. His toned chest pressed against my back as he once again held my arm and turned me around to face him. This time, he reached for my chin and forced me to look up into his eyes.

I gasped.

Those eyes were my complete undoing.

Gone was that frightening red, and in its place was a breathtaking emerald green.

Bewildered, I couldn't keep myself from spluttering, "Your... your eyes? Wha—?"

He looked as confused by my words as I felt. Turning around, he gazed at his reflection in a glass windshield. He stood frozen for several minutes. When he turned back to face me, he looked in a world of his own. His eyes had glazed over and his voice was hoarse as he spoke.

"Huh…"

I didn't understand how it could have happened, or what it meant. But each second I remained staring into those beautiful green eyes of his, I felt myself sliding further and further away from where I knew I needed to keep myself. I had been trying to detach myself from him, but now I couldn't find the strength to stop looking into his eyes.

"Well, I-I'm happy for you," I said.

I flinched beneath his steady gaze.

"I'd just like a simple answer."

"Why?"

He paused and I could see that he was choosing his next words carefully. It cut me to see how uncomfortable I was making this for him.

"We—"

"*We?*" I hissed. "There is no *we*. There never has been any—"

My voice broke. My heart pounded and blood rushed furiously to my face. I began to sweat.

And then I lost all control.

"I have feelings for nobody!" I screamed, my throat stinging. "Irina fell for Adrian. That's all that ever happened!"

I was horrified by the words as soon as they had escaped my lips. As soon as I realized how they sounded out loud. I fell to my knees, covering my face with my hands, every part of my body shaking.

His body brushed against mine as he lowered himself down onto the floor next to me, leaning against the bench alongside me. I raised my eyes to his and as I did, more passion coursed through me than I knew how to handle. Attempting to stifle my emotions would have been like trying to extinguish a forest fire with dry wood.

I had lost all sense of what was right and wrong. All I had left was my rapidly beating heart exploding in my chest. Beating to break free from its cage.

As I reached both hands to his face, brushing my fingers against his skin, there was no way I could pretend that I was Irina.

I was Mona.

I knelt higher so that my face was level with his. He held my waist and stood up, pulling me back to my feet with him.

"That's all that ever happened," he repeated, his voice husky.

He brushed the tears away from my eyes with his thumbs, still staring at me.

My shoulders sagged.

There was no point denying it any longer.

He'd seen the truth in me.

The intensity of his gaze was now too much to bear. I closed my eyes and as soon as I did, my lips found his. His kiss was cautious, slow, at first. Exploring the contours of my lips, before requiring more. I grasped his hair, and pulled myself closer, closing the gap between us. Taking hold of my waist, he lifted me up against him so that he could reach all of me. His hands slid down beneath my thighs, his grip around them growing tighter with each second that passed.

It was only once I forced my lips away from his that the inevitable pain I knew would come began tearing through my chest.

I ran out of the shelter—something I cursed myself for not doing to begin with—and jumped into the water. I sprinted across the beach as fast as my weak legs could carry me toward the gate. Kiev caught up with me as soon as I'd stepped through the gate. He held a parasol in one hand, gripping my arm with the other.

I whirled around and glared up at him.

"Let go of me," I breathed, even while my heart burst. "I don't want to ever see your face again."

He stepped back, the expression on his face tearing me apart. As I disappeared into the shade of the forest, he didn't follow me. Thorns cut my feet as I ran. Biting my lip, I relished the pain. I wanted more of it. I dug my nails into my right arm and scratched until I'd etched a deep cut. Blood flowed. And I wished that it flowed more. Because it distracted me from recalling his expression. It distracted me from his memory. From the bonfire in my heart.

I thought I could hide behind my childish games. I thought I could trick fate, trick destiny, with some stupid act. What a damn fool I've been.

I barged through my front door, ran to the desk and, scrambling in the drawers, took out the story. The story that I had once so dearly cherished. The story that I now hated with every fiber of my being. In a wild rage, page by page, I ripped the parchment to pieces, and with it, my heart ripped too.

But I didn't care.

I needed my heart to be ripped.

I needed it to stop feeling. To stop beating.

I needed it to be numb.

"Numbness."

Once my floor was covered in shreds, I gathered them together and hurled them in the lake. As they shrivelled up, tears flowed more heavily from my eyes. Angrily, I brushed them aside.

If it hadn't been for that story, Kai would never have died. I wouldn't have had to let Evie go.

And Kiev never would have kissed Mona.

It wasn't fair that I'd allowed him to do it. He didn't know the price that came with that kiss. If he had known, he never would have claimed it.

He didn't know why I'd had to watch my family—parents, sisters, brothers, and cousins—die when I was a young girl.

He didn't know why I'd been banished from my own realm.

He didn't know why I'd never known romance.

I had fooled myself that perhaps the curse had passed over me. That perhaps I was unnecessarily restricting myself from living. I had dared to hope. Dared to dream. And in entertaining such foolish notions, I'd become complacent. In trying to finish that stupid story, I'd let myself climb out of my cage. When I should have kept the lock fastened and thrown away the key.

But then my baby Kai had died.

And I'd known then that the chain had been set off again.

Now I feared that it was only a matter of time.

I have to leave this place.

As the last bloodstained shreds of Adrian and Irina's story drowned beneath the water lilies, I just prayed that the damage hadn't already been done.

Ready for the next part of Kiev and Mona's story?

A Shade of Kiev 2 is available now!

Visit: www.bellaforrest.net for more information.

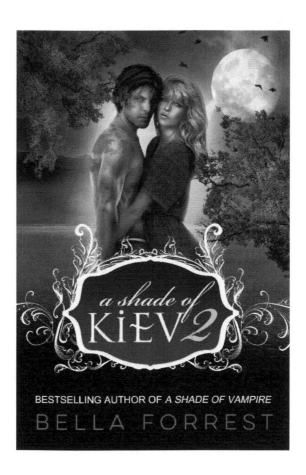

Further note from the author

If you would like to learn more about Kiev, and you haven't yet read my *A Shade of Vampire* series, I suggest you read it because it's where Kiev's story started. You'll also get a deeper understanding of the world in which he now finds himself.

Printed in Great Britain
by Amazon.co.uk, Ltd.,
Marston Gate.